COCK TALES

COCK TALES

BOB VICKERY

Leyland Publications
San Francisco

First edition 1997
COCK TALES is copyright © 1997 by Bob Vickery.

Front cover photo copyright © 1997 by Kristen Bjorn
Cover design by Rupert Kinnard

Library of Congress Cataloging-in-Publication Data

Vickery, Bob.
    Cock tales / Bob Vickery.—1st ed.
    159 p. 22 cm.
    ISBN 0-943595-65-7
    1. Gay men—Sexual behavior—Fiction.   2. Erotic stories,
American.   I. Title.
PS3572.I256C63   1997
813'.54—dc21   97-11100
                                                              CIP

Leyland Publications
P.O. Box 410690
San Francisco, CA 94141
Complete illustrated catalogue available for $1 ppd.

CONTENTS

UNCUT SPLENDOR

I'T'S NOT A GOOD idea to mix business with pleasure, especially out in the field. It can lead to all sorts of complications. Like unemployment. But it happened to me once, about a year ago at a copper mine in Arizona. A small operation, no more than a few dozen workers, just the kind of place where you can find drums of hazardous waste tucked in some corner, corroded, rusted and leaking a toxic witch's brew into the ground. I flashed my Bureau of Mining credentials at the front desk and had the foreman give me the tour. He was a short guy, just barely came up to my shoulder, with stubby legs, a powerful torso, and huge fuckin' arms. He wasn't stupid, by any means; he knew the mining operation cold and answered the questions I fired at him with an easy confidence. But something about the slope of his forehead, his wide mouth, and the way his eyes glittered under his thick brows gave him the look of an intelligent ape, dressed up in a pin-striped shirt and tie and wearing a hard-hat.

I was trying to be professional, goddammit, asking him where the mine shipped its wastes, what personnel were trained to handle it, what the emergency procedures were in case of a spill, all that stuff, but there was this undercurrent going on between us. He answered my questions all right, but with this grin on his face, his eyes bright and amused. And beneath the amusement . . . interest. He liked flexing his arms, letting me see the ripple of muscle under his tight shirt. Something a goddamn teenager would do. And I was eating it up! You got to realize, when I tour the mines I'm out on the road for a couple of weeks. That means nights in motels watching T.V., greasy chicken in chain restaurants, and then back on the road again until I get to the next mine. It can be lonely work.

When the inspection was over (the place was clean) I shook his hand and said goodbye, he'd get my report in three or four weeks, but there was nothing to sweat over. He flashed this wide grin and said, *Before you go, there's something you should see*, and steered me behind the main building to a corrugated tin storage shed. *What's to see?* I asked, staring at him in the dim light streaming down from the slits where the roof met the walls. *This*, he said, yanking his pants down, setting free this monster ape dick, long and thick as a baby's arm, with a swollen, red head whose cumslit was already oozing jizz. Well, I was down on my knees before I even had time to think about it, slobbering over his dick, deep-throatin' it, burying my nose in his black, crinkly pubes while his cockhead hammered against the back of my throat. I slid my hands under his shirt, kneading the hard muscles of his torso, squeezing his nipples viciously as he plowed his fat dick in and out of my mouth. I felt his body tremble, and I gave an extra tug on his tits. He groaned mightily and pulled his dick out of my mouth just as it started squirting, pelting my face with his load. I could feel his dick slime slowly ooze down my face as I knelt in front of him in that hot, airless shed, my shirt plastered to my back, the sweat trickling down my sides. I wiped my bare hand across my face and started fucking my fist, now greased with his jizz. He looked down at me, grinning, his pants around his ankles, his thick cock slowly sinking, his balls heavy and ripe in the heat. It only took a couple of seconds before I felt my own load pulled up from my balls, ready to shoot. I threw back my head and let 'er rip, my spunk shooting out onto the dusty floor. *Fuckin' A!* he crooned, as I shook out the last drop. He bent down and planted his mouth over mine, pushing his tongue deep down my throat, and then helped me to my feet. A couple of minutes later he walked me to my car and I drove off, his muscular little body framed in my rear view mirror.

I'm thinking about that incident now, because I'm sitting in the front office of the Yellow Rose Gold Mine, a year later and six hundred miles further west, fantasizing about history repeating itself. The company engineer is describing the operation of the mine to me. I didn't catch his first name, something that starts with a "J" (Jeff? Jim?) but his last name is Sandalaw, I see it on the I.D. badge pinned to his crisp, neatly pressed white shirt. Sandalaw is walking me through the gold extraction process of this mine step by step. I'm staring at him as he speaks, feeling my body following its own agenda: the rapid flutter of the pulse, that constriction of the throat, and the slow, serpentine expansion and hardening of my dick that lets me know this guy is seriously making my gonads churn. I'd say he's a couple of years older than me, early thirties maybe, red hair just long enough to put a part in it, light blue eyes, and a trim body whose muscularity is just hinted at beneath the tight white shirt and tie that is the typical engineer's uniform. It's the freckles that do me in. They run across the bridge of his nose and up and down his muscular forearms like specks of light brown paint. Huck Finn with a mining geology degree. Sandalaw describes how the arsenic solution leaches through the slag mounds to extract the gold, and he's fuckin' breaking my heart. I'm such a sucker for the confident, cleancut masculinity of this field technician. There's a gold wedding ring on his finger, and I picture him plowing his wife early in the morning before setting out for work, those freckled hands stroking her breasts, his smooth, white ass pumping up and down with each thrust of his dick . . .

"Would you like to inspect the site now?" Sandalaw asks me. His eyes regard me with a level gaze. There's nothing hostile about his attitude, but there's a no-nonsense quality about him that demands an equally serious response.

"Sure," I say. "Let's go to it."

We step outside the air conditioned office and the heat hits us like a sledge hammer. We are twenty-seven miles southwest of Death Valley as the buzzard flies, and it's hotter than the Devil's asshole right now. I slip on my shades as does Sandalaw, and we pile into his four-wheel drive. He takes me over the slag mounds, alongside the excavation pits, past the cyanide leaching ponds and the carbon filtration units. Our conversation is almost entirely limited to the mining operation, but every now and then it hits a personal note. Sandalaw tells me he's married with two kids, both girls, and that his family lives in Boron, the nearest town. I tell him I'm staying at the Motel 6 there and will be flying back to the home office in Denver tomorrow. I find a couple of minor violations, nothing worth writing up; Sandalaw says he'll make sure they get corrected before the shift is over. I ask for a business card, and he pulls one out of his wallet and hands it to me. Glancing at it, I see his first name is Jesse. *Jesse*, I repeat to myself. A sexy name. We shake hands, and when we do this he smiles for the first time, his teeth flashing white in his tanned face.

I'm seized by a sudden impulse. "Is there any night life in Boron?" I ask. "I'm not looking forward to the idea of hanging out in my motel room all night."

Jesse thinks about this. "You might try The Silver Lode. It's just a crummy little bar with a couple of pool tables. Guys at the mine here hang out there sometimes. Bikers like it too when they pass through."

I thank him, he says *Don't mention it*, I climb into my rental car and drive off.

I walk through the door of The Silver Lode. Though I've never been to Boron before, I've lost count how many times I've been in this bar. Whether it's Carson City, Bakersfield, Yuma, Flagstaff, or one of any number of other cities I've passed through on my inspections, the damn bars are always the same: the flickering neon sign in the window with one letter burnt out, the cigarette haze, the human relics on the bar stools, the pool table in the back. I'm wearing my old frayed jeans, a white T-shirt, and my duckbill cap that reads *Bureau of Mines* along the front. I buy a Bud and grab a table. Johnny Cash is singing *Ring of Fire* on the jukebox. The only place less appealing than here is my motel room.

I get up and put a quarter on the edge of the pool table to claim the next game. One of the good ol' boys playing glances at my cap and then gives me a long, sour look. "We already got players lined up for the rest of the night," he says, his voice as flat as road kill.

I take the hint and return to my table, keeping my expression cool even though I'm steaming inside. It's my damn cap, with "Bureau of Mines" stitched in it. I got to remember never to wear this out in the field again; I keep forgetting how much "the heartland" hates government workers. I decide to finish my beer and then go back to the motel and watch one of the cable porno movies. A couple of geezers are playing Liar's Dice at the bar; everyone else is drinking in silence. Johnny's done with his song, and the only sounds in the place are the slap of the dice cup against the bar and the click of pool balls. I couldn't get more depressed. I take one last swig from my beer and push back my chair.

The door opens and Jesse walks in. He sees me at the table, nods at me and gets a beer at the bar. After a couple of minutes he joins me. "I was wondering if you'd be here," he says.

"You caught me just as I was leaving," I say.

Jesse grins. He's loosened up quite a bit since the mine inspection. "Oh, yeah? What are you going to do, hang out in your motel room all night?" He glances over at the guy behind the bar. "Jimmy," he calls out, "Another beer for my friend."

I take him all in: the boyish grin, the level, blue eyes, the muscles of his body pushing out against his tight T-shirt. *What the hell*, I think, settling back into my chair. "You don't have to be so damn friendly, you know," I say. "Your mine passed the inspection anyway."

Jesse laughs. "Maybe I just want a little company tonight." He slouches down in his seat, his arms crossed against his chest. I watch his biceps bunch up. "My wife's visiting her mother over at Lake Havasu. She took the kids with her, and the house is feeling empty. I thought I'd hang out here for a while, soak up a little friendly atmosphere." He turns to the bar. "Jimmy," he calls out. "Where's that damn beer?" Underneath all the high spirits, there's something a little manic about the guy. Jimmy finally comes with the beer and sets it down in front of me.

Jesse and I hang out. It doesn't take long before we graduate to pitchers of beer. The place gradually fills up; the jukebox is playing non-stop now and the din of people talking is getting deafening. My eyes are burning from the cigarette smoke that hangs in the air like swamp gas.

Every minute I spend with Jesse just makes me all the hornier. It's not just his looks, though God knows he is one sexy dude, with that tight, muscular body of his and his all-American face. It's this way he has about him. He sits there across the table, telling me something funny his little girl did in school and then throws his head back and laughs. He's got a fuckin' great laugh, easy and natural, full of good humor, and it makes him so goddamn beautiful my heart aches. I want to see him in bed naked. I let my mind drift with that image, giving Jesse a thick, meaty dick and a couple of juicy low-hangers. Jesse suddenly says something and I glance up to see him staring at me. I wonder how much of my thoughts were on my face.

"I'm sorry, I didn't hear you," I say.

Jesse leans forward. "Let's get out of here," he shouts in my ear. "This is no place to talk."

I glance at my watch. "Don't you have to work tomorrow?"

Jesse grimaces. "Fuck work. I'm feeling wired tonight. Let's go over to my place. I have a couple of six-packs in the refrigerator."

I have to check out by seven tomorrow and catch a plane in San Diego, and I think about calling it a night. But there's an edge to Jesse that's making me begin to wonder about him. Why does he want me to go back with him to his empty house? I give him a long, level look. Jesse seems to have trouble meeting my gaze. *The fucker's nervous*, I realize. *What's he trying to work himself up to?* I'd like to find out. "Okay," I say.

I follow Jesse in my rental down a series of dark streets to his house. He finally pulls up to a curb, and I park behind him. He lives in a split-level ranchhouse, nothing fancy, but about what you'd expect an engineer to be able to afford. There's a tricycle on the sidewalk and he kicks it aside. "I keep telling my kids to put their stuff away," he grumbles. His words have a slight slur to them; both of us are a few sheets to the wind. He fumbles with his key and pushes open the front door. I follow behind him into his living room.

"So do you want another beer?" he asks.

I'm feeling high but not drunk. "No, I've had enough."

Jesse laughs a little uncertainly. "Well, what was the point of coming over here if you don't want a beer?"

I look right into his eyes. "You tell me." I keep my face calm, but inside my heart is beating hard.

Jesse's eyes dart away and then return back towards me again. He's still wearing his grin, but it looks like an afterthought now. I can see that he wants it bad, his little walk on the wild side while the wife is out of town. I reach over and plant my mouth on his. Jesse misses a beat out of surprise, but in a second he's eagerly returning the kiss, his tongue pushing deep inside my mouth. I shove him against the wall and grind my pelvis hard against him. He's going wild now, his hands all over me, squeezing my ass, sliding up and down my back, slipping under my T-shirt and kneading my torso. I reach down and cup his dick with my hand, feeling its hardness under the rough fabric of his jeans. Jesse groans softly.

He starts tugging at my clothes, pulling my shirt up, unbuckling my belt, his mouth never leaving my face. I reach under his T-shirt and feel the smooth hardness of his torso. I give nis nipples a not-too-gentle squeeze as I shove my tongue deep down his throat. My dick is threatening to split my jeans open. He breaks free, gasping for air. "Sonuvabitch," he groans. I don't know if he's calling me one, or if that's just a general exclamation.

"You got a bedroom somewhere around here?" I ask.

"Yeah," Jesse pants. "Follow me."

We walk down a long hallway, dropping clothes behind us. By the time we fall onto his double bed, we're both buck naked. Jesse has the smooth, white skin of a redhead, sprayed with freckles everywhere. His body is lean and defined, every muscle etched sharply against his pale skin. Underneath a red-orange brush of pubic hair, his dick juts out in all its blood-engorged, uncut splendor. I pull Jesse to me and kiss him again, pressing my body tightly against his. He reaches down and wraps his hand around both our dicks and starts stroking them in unison. I watch our two dicks squeezed together, mine dark, thick and cut, his pink and fat, the cockhead flaring out and oozing pre-cum.

Jesse rolls on top of me and pins my arms down over my head. He arches his back and pumps his hips so that his dick is dry-humping my belly. His face looms above mine, the ache in his eyes so palpable I almost feel it as a slap. "Fuckin' hot naked man," he croons, "with his muscular, hairy body and that thick, big dick of his . . ."

"Jesse," I grin. "When was the last time you got it on with another man?"

Jesse seems surprised by my question. "Years," he finally says. "Not since I got married." He kisses me on the mouth with a tenderness that's almost embarrassing in its intimacy. "Tonight," he whispers, "I'm going to make up for lost time." He drags his tongue down my body, across my pectoral, and swirls it once around the nipple. Taking the nub between his teeth, he bites gently, not quite crossing the threshold into pain. At the same time his fingers lightly flicker across my balls and up the shaft of my dick. I shudder involuntarily, and Jesse looks up at me and grins. I'm truly surprised. I had expected Jesse to have the finesse of a bull in heat, that this would be a rough-and-tumble roll in the sack with some country cowboy. I hadn't anticipated this . . . subtlety.

I raise my head to kiss him, but Jesse plants his forearm against my chest and pushes me down against the bed. "Don't do anything," he says. "Just lie there and let me explore your body." He burrows his face between my pecs, nuzzling the hairs of my chest and then slides his tongue down across my abs. He wraps his hand around my cock but doesn't stroke it, just squeezes it gently. Suddenly, he bends my dick down and lets go; it slaps hard against my belly. Jesse does this again, and then a third time, like a kid with a new toy.

He shifts around until he's lying between the V of my legs, his face pushed up towards my crotch. It's a warm desert night, and my balls are heavy from the heat. Jesse buries his face into them and breathes deeply. I lay there with my hands beneath my head and watch all of this. I have never had my body treated with such . . . reverence. Jesse seems fascinated by my hairiness, my muscles, my *maleness*. I feel Jesse's tongue moisten my nutsac, tickle the hairs, and then he sucks both balls between his lips. He looks up at me, my scrotum in his mouth, and shoots me a look I can't read: satisfaction? bliss? excitement? His tongue rolls over my balls with increasing urgency, and I feel a small jolt of alarm. But, as with my nipples, he stops before crossing into pain.

His hands slide under my hips and cup my ass, kneading the cheek muscles, as his tongue slobbers up the shaft of my dick. His fingers pry apart my asscrack and rub against my bung hole with a feather's lightness. I wait for him to penetrate inside me, but his hands leave my ass and move all over my body now, squeezing and massaging my flesh, kneading the muscle.

He nibbles my dickhead, swirling the fleshy knob with his tongue. Suddenly his mouth swoops down the shaft at the same moment that he squeezes my nipples *hard*. I cry out and involuntarily thrust my hips up, shoving my dick deep down his throat. He takes it all in and I begin the serious business of fucking this boy's face, pumping my hips in quick, staccato thrusts as I pummel the back of his throat. Jesse can't get enough of my dick; as hard as I plow his mouth, he seems hungry for more. He swings his head from side to side, sucks hard, and rolls his tongue over my shaft in a way that's pushing me to the brink mighty fuckin' fast. I want to hold off, make it last, but Jesse is having none of that. His mouth is a force of nature, implacable as a tornado, and I'm just some damn trailer park in its path. I fall back onto the bed with my arms out wide. When the orgasm finally explodes, I shoot my load down Jesse's throat, crying out like some lost soul from hell.

Jesse looks up and gives me a spermy smile. "Sit on my chest," I growl. "And drop your balls in my mouth." Jesse's grin widens. In no time at all, I'm sucking on his nuts as he slaps his dick against my face, rubbing it on my cheeks, my nose, my eyes. He spits in his hand and slides it up and down his fat, freckled cock as I roll his ballsac around with my tongue. I worm a finger up Jesse's ass and twist it. Jesse throws back his head and groans. I shove my finger up another knuckle, pushing hard against his prostate, and Jesse's whole body shudders. He groans again, louder and then his load pulses out of his dick and splatters against my face, one squirt, then another, and another after that. I feel the thick, ropy strands of his wad slide down my cheeks. Jesse bends down and licks my face clean, ending with his mouth on mine. He collapses down beside me, and we lay there in his bed, flank to flank; I feel his body rise and fall with every breath he takes. A couple of minutes go by in silence, and then Jesse rolls over on top of me and plants his mouth on mine again.

We spend most of the night trying every goddamn position ever thought of by man, and a couple more to boot. I have never had a partner as insatiable as Jesse; and yet every time he plows my ass again, or jacks off in my face, or sucks my dick, there's this look of *exhilaration* on his face, as intense and fresh as the first time. Even when the clock on his night table reads 4:10 and my body is screaming for a break so that I can get some *sleep*, Jesse's head is burrowed between my legs, his mouth trying to coax forth one last load.

I have to push him away. "Jesse, please," I beg. "Enough is enough."

Jesse gives me this smile, and I swear he looks like a choir boy. He slides up next to me and kisses me lightly on the mouth. "Like I said," he murmurs. "I was just making up for lost time." He turns out the light and wraps his arms around me. I sink into his embrace and drift off into sleep.

It seems like I've just closed my eyes when Jesse's alarm goes off. Jesse lies naked in the bed, watching me as I pull on my clothes like a zombie. He doesn't have to report to the mine for another hour, but I have to return to the motel and check out.

"So I guess there'll be no reason for you to come back to Boron, soon, will there?" he asks. I can't read the expression on his face.

I shake my head. "Not for at least a year," I say. "There are a lot of mines out there and only a handful of inspectors. I can't even guarantee they'll pick me to inspect The Yellow Rose, when it's time again." Neither one of us say anything else as I tie my shoes. I finally glance up at him. "How you doing?" I ask, running my hand up his calf.

Jesse shrugs but says nothing. "I'm all right," he finally says. "I love my wife. And I do like women. I just like guys, too." He gives a little laugh. "I just wish you mining inspectors would come by a little more often."

"Christ," I grin. "If we did, you'd fuck us all to death."

When I'm ready to leave, Jesse walks with me to the door. He pulls me in his arms and we give each other a long, very wet kiss. "See you next year," he says. "With a little luck."

Out on the road I can see the sun in my rear view mirror, hanging over the horizon, throwing long shadows every time I pass by a billboard or rock outcropping. It's still early, and I'm the only car on the road. The highway cuts straight across the desert and disappears into the horizon. I speed down it with nothing but Jesse on my mind. Sleep deprivation and the strangeness of the desert landscape make me feel like I'm driving through a dream. There's nothing but country-western on the radio, so I settle back and listen to Clint Black sing as my car eats up the miles to home.

WALTZ FUCK

THE MINUTE I see the landlady's face, I know I'm in for a rough time. I've seen friendlier faces on America's Most Wanted.

"I came to see about the furnished apartment you got for rent," I say.

Her eyes slide up and down my body quicker than a gateman's at a high priced night club. I just got off my shift at my cousin Vinnie's garage and I'm wearing my old, greasy coveralls. Five seconds after we meet, she's got me pigeon-holed good, and I know it isn't under the heading "Likely Prospects."

"First and last month's rent, plus $150 deposit," she says flatly.

I feel a little flicker of anger flare up at her attitude, but I quench it quick. I'm new in town and need a place bad. I can't hold up much longer sleeping in a Motel 6, not with what Vinnie's paying me. "Can I see the apartment?" I ask politely.

She gives me another poisonous look and pulls a ring of keys from off a nail by the door. "Follow me," she mutters.

I tag after her as we climb three flights of stairs. By the time we're at the third floor, she's wheezing bad. Maybe that's why she's so pissed off at having to show the place. She staggers over to a door, unlocks it, and opens it, without saying a word. I walk in. The place is a studio, bigger than your average steamer trunk, but not by much. The carpeting is torn to hell and stained, and whatever color the walls were painted originally, I'm sure they hadn't started out as the puke yellow they are now. The apartment has only one thing going for it: it looks affordable.

I walk across the room and look out the window, beyond the fire escape. There's a tiny yard covered with brown, beaten-down grass, and a board fence. On the other side is a cemetery. It's pretty small, just a couple of hills covered with tombstones that seem to come right down to the property line. Near the top of the closer hill, a man is standing knee deep digging a grave, a pile of damp dirt beside him. I wonder about what it'd be like seeing a bunch of graves every time I look out the window. Hell, I tell myself, it's just a park with tombstones and it's better this than facing a noisy city street.

I turn to the landlady. "What's the rent?" I ask.

She looks at me as if trying to decide whether or not to take me seriously. "$250 a month," she says. "Utilities not included."

"Okay, it's a deal," I say. "I want to move in tonight."

She blinks in surprise. "First and last month's rent, plus $150 deposit," is all she manages to come up with.

"Yeah, you already told me," I reply. I sit on the bed and write her a check, hoping I can hit Vinnie up for an advance on my pay to make it good. I hand it to her. The mattress I'm sitting on feels like a sack of rocks. "Any chance you can come up with another mattress?" I ask.

"Anything extra will cost you extra," she says. She hands me a set of keys and walks out the door. I can tell we're going to get on like gangbusters. Still, it's a relief to have a place. I can't get out of that damn motel soon enough.

I walk over to the window and look out at the cemetery again. The grave digger is now up to his thighs in the hole. I watch him stab the ground with his shovel, swing his arms high and let the dirt fly. He's giving himself a good workout; his pits are stained with sweat and his T-shirt is plastered to his back. He pauses for a second and peels his shirt off. His chest is matted with black hair, but that doesn't hide the cut of the pecs or how hard his belly is. His biceps bunch nicely with each thrust of the shovel, and when he twists his torso to toss the dirt, the muscles in his back ripple in a way that tightens my throat up. With his thick black hair and moustache, and his dark skin, he looks like a Greek sailor, or maybe an Italian gondolier. He looks fuckin' beautiful.

A few minutes later he's done with the hole. He grabs his T-shirt, slings his shovel over his shoulder like a soldier's rifle, and strolls up the hill, disappearing over the crest. I stand there staring at the open grave for a few seconds, my hands jammed in my pockets.

I move in that afternoon. It doesn't take long, just going over to the motel and piling my clothes and Jim's weight set into my car. I still think of the weight set as Jim's; it's the only thing of his I've kept. I spend my first night out on the fire escape, smoking cigarettes. The moon's almost full tonight. I know graveyards are supposed to be spooky in moonlight, but I don't feel that way at all. Actually, it's nice and peaceful; the tombstones look like buildings in a small city, and I fantasize about taking a walk among them, like Godzilla on a stroll. Only the open grave makes me feel a little creepy. All I see in it is black, and from the fire escape it looks like the hole could go on down for miles. I imagine dropping into the grave and falling down into the blackness, never hitting bottom. After a while I climb through the window back into my apartment and go to bed.

When I come home from work the next day, there's a funeral going on. The mourners are gathered around the grave that the grave digger dug yesterday. The hole doesn't seem bottomless anymore; in fact I can see the top of the coffin lying in it, with what looks like a wreath of roses and lilies on top of it. I open the refrigerator for a beer; that plus my vials of AZT are the only things in there. I really got to do some shopping. I'm curious about the ceremony. After a couple of minutes I climb out onto the fire escape, a beer in hand, to get a better view. The grave is close enough that I have something of a ringside seat. A hefty lady with legs like a linebacker's stands on the edge of the grave sobbing. A young man (her son?) stands next to her, his hands clasped together in front, his face as stony as the marble angel's on the tomb a few plots away. There's a gust of wind, and a lock of dark hair falls against his forehead. He impatiently brushes it away. His dark suit is cut nicely, showing off the broad shoulders and the tall, lean body to good advantage. As the priest drones on, the young man looks around, obviously bored. For a second our eyes meet. His mouth pulls down into a scowl and he gives me the evil eye. I guess I can't blame him; I must look like some kind of rubbernecker sitting up on the fire escape, watching them all between sips of beer. I look away, but I don't go back inside until after the last of the mourners has walked away.

I strip off my greasy overalls and step into the shower. I feel in a weird mood: restless, edgy, like the idle of my choke is set too high. Maybe it's because of the funeral. The last funeral I went to was Jim's, and some sleeping dogs are threatening to rise now. I stand under the shower head and let the hot water beat against my face, keeping my mind blank. Unexpectedly, the image of the young mourner flashes into my head, and with it a surge of lust as violent and unexpected as a bolt of lightning. My dick swells to full erection and I wrap my soapy hand around it, stroking it slowly. I stop short of shooting. I turn the water off and walk out of the bathroom, toweling myself off. The light from outside is dimming as the late afternoon sinks into evening. I flip the wall switch on. I'm aware that I'm buck naked in a room with no curtains, but who's out there to see me, the stiffs in their graves?

I put the towel behind my back and rub, feeling my still half-hard dick swing heavily from side to side. When was the last time I got laid? I thought. Too long. I got to meet some guys in this town, get a sex life going for me again. Maybe tonight I'll hit a couple of bars and see if I get lucky.

A movement outside in the cemetery catches my eye. It's the grave digger, filling in the grave. I wrap the towel around my waist and walk up to the window to watch. He stands on the edge of the hole, shoveling the dirt in with a quick, easy swing of his arms. With the setting of the sun, the day has cooled down; he's got a red flannel shirt on, this time, but it's unbuttoned, and I grab the opportunity to check out his fine body again. I take in the hairy chest, the torn, mud-smeared jeans, the muscular forearms that extend down from the rolled-up sleeves, and my dick makes a little tent against the terry-cloth of my towel. Where is all this horniness coming from? I wonder. Yesterday the grave digger reminded me of an Italian gondolier. Today, the impression is darker, even a little menacing. Watching him toss the dirt inside the hole I can't imagine him doing any other line of work than what he's doing now: burying bodies.

He puts the shovel down to rest for a while, and when he raises his head, our eyes meet. We look at each other for a few beats; in the dimming light it's impossible to read his expression. Eventually, he goes back to his shovel and continues filling in the grave. But a few seconds later he looks back up at me again. I stand there without moving, my left arm raised and pressed against the side of the window, my weight leaning against it. He goes on shoveling, but always, every few seconds, raising his head and glancing up at me. I feel my heart pounding. After a few more minutes, the hole is filled and he tamps the dirt down with the blade of his shovel. He looks back at me one last time and then disappears beyond the crest of the hill.

That night I dream I'm in a coffin that must be made of glass, because I can see through it. I'm in a grave, surrounded by high banks of dirt. A figure stands at the edge of the hole, looking down at me. It's the mourner I saw yesterday; except for a black arm-band around his left bicep, he's naked. At first his face is as ex-pressionless as it was at yesterday's funeral, but when he sees me staring at him, his lips curve up into an easy smile. He wraps his hand around his dick and starts jerking off with slow, regular strokes.

The grave digger walks up to the other side of the grave, equally naked. His dick juts straight out, and his balls hang loose and heavy, just above the crack of his ass. I've never seen a naked male body from this perspective before, and it excites the hell out of me. He carries his shovel over his shoulder in his usual way. Like the mourner, he starts stroking his dickmeat, and I watch as his balls swing in tempo to his beating off. The two of them lean over the grave and kiss, their mouths fused together in a long, wet liplock. I stare up at the two torsos bent over me, struck by the contrast: the mourner's smooth, pale body against the grave digger's dark hairiness. As if on cue, they both quicken the speed of their strokes. Their bodies are soaked with sweat; drops of it splash against the top of my coffin. After a while, the mourner's body begins to shud-der. He throws back his head and cries out, as he squirts a load into the grave. The grave digger is soon doing the same, his knees buckled and his hairy chest heaving. He roars like a bull in pain. The jizz from both men comes splattering down on top of my coffin in thick, spermy gobs. The grave digger shakes the last few drops out of his dick and winks at the mourner. He shifts his shovel to both hands and, with slow, precise thrusts, begins fill-ing in the grave. In a matter of seconds, I'm completely buried.

I wake up with my heart hammering. After a while, when it's obvious I'm not going to fall back to sleep, I get up and walk around the room. Looking out the window, I can just barely make out the new grave in the moonlight. I feel my belly turn over. I spend the next couple of hours working out at Jim's weight set so hard that by the time I finally crawl back to bed I can barely lift my arms.

The next day, after I get home from work, I see that the grave digger is working on a new hole. He looks up immediately as I approach the window. I get the feeling he's been waiting for me. Once again, I feel my throat constrict. I move away from the window, out of his line of sight. I try to think about the best way of handling this. Eventually I go into the kitchen and get a couple of beers from the refrigerator. I climb out onto the fire escape. The grave digger is staring at me without any pretense of subtlety.

"Howdy," I call out to him.

The grave digger leans on his shovel. "Hi," he calls back in a deep baritone. Just like the first time I saw him, he's shirtless, and his muscular torso is streaked with sweat and dirt.

I hold a can of beer out to him. "You look thirsty. Wanna beer?"

He keeps looking at me, but says nothing for a couple of beats. Finally he grins, and the white of his teeth flashes in sharp contrast against his dark face. "Sure," he calls.

"Come down by the fence," I shout.

The grave digger drops his shovel and descends the small hill. When he's almost at the bottom, I pull my arm back and toss the beer with a snap. The can arcs through the air, glinting in the light of the sun, and just clears the fence. The grave digger runs down the rest of the hill and catches it skillfully. He pulls back the tab, and a spray of foam spews out onto his face and torso. We both laugh. He toasts me with the can and chugs down what's left. I watch as the beer foam drips through his chest hairs and runs down onto his belly. When he's done, he tosses the can and climbs back up the hill. He continues with his digging, but a minute doesn't go by without his looking up at me. I lean against the wall of the building, warmed from the afternoon sun, and watch him with a deceptive laziness. After about half an hour he's done. He slings his shovel over his shoulder, but before he walks off, he turns again towards me. "What's your name?" he calls out to me.

"Tim," I call back.

"I'll come back later tonight. Around ten. If you want it, meet me here." He climbs to the top of the hill and disappears over the edge.

I can't quite believe that I heard him right. I tell myself that there's no way I'm going to be lurking in a graveyard in the dark, like some damn ghoul. But for the rest of the evening I can't take my eyes off the window for more than a minute. A few minutes before ten I'm clambering down the fire escape and over the board wall as if I'd been planning this all along.

There's a cloud hiding the moon, and I have to grope my way between the tombstones. It's a warm night tonight, with a slight breeze. I can hear the sounds of traffic off in the distance, but here it's quiet and still. With what light there is, the tombstones made of marble gleam faintly. After a while, I sit on a granite headstone adjacent to the open grave and wait. I close my eyes and breathe deeply, trying to calm down.

"Hello, Tim," a voice says behind me. I jump up, with a sharp inrush of breath. The grave digger steps out of the shadow of a cypress tree.

"Jeez," I say. "How long have you been standing there?"

The grave digger walks up to me. "Not long." He smiles. "I didn't know if you'd make it or not."

His smile isn't altogether reassuring. There's something more than a little wolfish about it. "I didn't know either," I say. "It just sort of happened." I give a nervous laugh. "I wasn't sure whether or not you'd come either."

The cloud covering the moon passes away, and the grave digger's face is suddenly bathed in light. His smile broadens and his teeth gleam. "Oh, I'm going to come tonight," he says. "You can bet your life on it." He pulls me over to him and plants his mouth on mine. His tongue works its way into my mouth and thrusts deep inside. I suck on it greedily, my hands slipping under his T-shirt and across the bare skin of his torso. I pinch his nipples hard, and he gives out a long, trailing groan. He cups my ass with his hands and pulls my body against his. We grind our torsos together, dry fucking each other with slow, circular thrusts of our hips. I can feel the hardness of his dick against the rough fabric of his jeans.

He raises his arms as I peel his shirt off, and I get a whiff of fresh sweat. I bury my face in the nearest pit, inhaling deeply. The acrid/sweet smell fills my head, and I slide my tongue down his torso, till my mouth engulfs his left nipple. I run my tongue over it, feeling it harden. Taking it between my teeth I nip it gently. He gives out a long sigh, just shy of a groan. I trail my tongue across the hairs of his chest and work over the right nipple as well. His hands slide down my back and slip under my jeans. I feel the callouses of his palms rub roughly against the skin of my ass.

I step into the open grave so that my face is level with his crotch. I run my tongue across the front of his jeans, tasting the dried mud and grit accumulated from the day's digging. I can feel his dick push up against the fabric, and I work my mouth against it, wetting the cloth with my saliva. He unbuckles his belt; I open his fly and pull his jeans down around his ankles. His dick springs out at full attention. It gleams in the moonlight, the head red and flared. The balls hang low and fleshly, swollen like ripe fruit. I bury my face in them and inhale deeply, breathing in their sharp, musky odor.

I wrap my hand around the grave digger's cock and squeeze gently; a spermy pearl oozes out and I lap it up. The warmth of his dick spreads across my palm. I run my tongue along the shaft teasingly, flicking it lightly as my hands continue to move across his torso. I take his dick into my mouth and nibble my lips down its length. His body trembles beneath my fingertips, and his breath takes on a harsh, rasping quality, like some large animal struggling.

He places his hands alongside my head and begins pumping his hips. I twist my head from side to side to increase the sensation of my lips sliding along his dickmeat and he groans his appreciation. With both hands I grab an ass cheek and squeeze. I can feel them tense and relax with each thrust of his dick down my throat.

I work a finger into the crack of his ass and rub it against his bung hole. I look up at his face, washed in moonlight, as I slowly penetrate his sphincter with my index finger. He returns my gaze with feverish eyes and another groan escapes from his open mouth. I work my finger up his ass to the third knuckle and begin fingerfucking him in a slow, steady tempo that matches the way he fucks my mouth. His legs tremble against my body like trees in a stiff wind.

He pulls his dick out of my mouth. "Get naked," he orders, his voice urgent. I kick off my shoes and pull off my shirt and pants. "The socks, too," he says. "I don't want any clothes on you." I pull them off too. There's a gust of breeze and I shiver slightly. The grave digger stands naked above me, legs apart, his dick jutting sharply over me. Last night's dream comes back to me with a sudden vividness. He squats down until his scrotum dangles above my face. "Eat my balls," he orders.

I place my mouth on them and kiss them lightly, the scrotum

hairs tickling my face. I bathe his nuts with my tongue, and then open my mouth wide, sucking them in. I reach up and run my hands over his torso. He slaps my face with his dick with a sharp *thwack* and then rubs it over my cheeks, my eyes, my nose.

He pulls away and steps into the grave with me. He wraps his arms around me tight and lowers me on my back. As in a trance, I let him determine the actions. Grabbing my jeans, he stuffs them behind my head to make a rough pillow, and then stretches out full on top of me, his mouth planted on mine. His body writhes against me with a slow, heavy sensuality. I raise my arm and accidentally brush against the side of the grave. Dirt sprinkles my face and the back of his head.

He lifts his hips and his dick begins poking in the crack of my ass. "Wait a second," I whisper. I reach behind me and fish out a condom from my jeans pocket. He watches silently as I roll it down the length of his shaft. He slicks his dick up with spit and then with excruciating slowness impales my ass. I gasp and close my eyes, feeling the fullness of his dick slide into me. He begins to pump his hips, fucking me in a grinding, hypnotic rhythm that is as stately as a waltz. Each thrust drives me deeper into the dirt; I can feel the gravel and gritty mud rake my back, working their way up into the crack of my ass. His body presses down on me like all the weight of the world and his hot breath rasps across my face. The sides of the grave seem to close in on me and I'm suddenly swept up by a wave of claustrophobia. I look up and see the full moon caught in the branches of the cypress tree. I breathe deep and focus on the moon. Eventually the panic passes. The grave digger has his strong arms wrapped around me as he plows my ass, and I slide into the warmth of his embrace. I thrust my hips up and match the rhythm of his strokes. He groans his gratitude, and my dick throbs with the knowledge of the pleasure I'm giving him.

The grave digger's groans become louder, more ragged. Little whimpers escape from him. I reach down and feel his balls; they're pulled up tight against his body, ready to shoot. He pumps his hips faster now, with a more driving force and I match him thrust for thrust. I reach up and twist his nipples hard and his body shudders convulsively. He raises his head and bellows. I can feel his throbbing dick squirt out load after load of jizz into the condom up my ass. I pull him down and kiss him hard, biting his lips. As our bodies rock together against the grave walls, dirt rains down on us. I'm stroking my own dick furiously and it's just seconds later before my own load pulses out of me, gushing onto my belly in thick, spermy puddles. The grave digger gives one last, trailing groan and then collapses on me. We lay there in the grave for God knows how long. The moon has passed out of sight, beyond the grave walls, and everything is dark.

The grave digger eventually stirs and rises to his feet. He climbs out of the grave and squats down, offering me his hand. I take it and he pulls me out back into the night air. A breeze blows through and I shiver. "Put your clothes back on," he says softly. "It's getting cold."

We dress in silence. When we're done, he pulls me to him and kisses me again. "I'll be back," he murmurs. "This is just a taste of things to come."

"I know," I whisper.

He turns and walks away and after a few steps disappears behind the hill. I stand there alone in the cemetery and breathe in the night air, grateful for the open space around me. The breeze blows again, brisker this time, and I shiver once more. I climb over the board fence and up the fire escape back to the warmth and security of my apartment. In bed I think about the next time, when I'll feel the grave digger's calloused hands on my body again, his hot breath on my face. I close my eyes and sleep the sleep of the dead.

IRON MAN

I T'S A LITTLE after eleven o'clock, late enough to draw a decent
bar crowd, but early enough, if I'm lucky, to score and still catch
a few hours sleep. I have to be in the hiring hall by eight o'clock
sharp tomorrow morning if I'm to get a crack at a job. It's crazy
to be cruising on a weekday night, but I haven't been laid since
I've moved out here and my cock is giving me a hard time about
it. Springsteen is playing on the juke box, and the boys are lined
up against the walls, checking out any new action that walks
through the door. I feel their eyes draw a bead on me, and it's
gratifying to see how they track me as I push my way through the
crowd. I need a little tender loving tonight; I'm feeling lonely and
more than a little depressed about not finding work.

I make my way to the bar and order the cheapest beer they got,
which is still three goddamn dollars. As I pull the bills from my
wallet, I realize that I'm going to have to nurse this sucker for the
rest of the night. That is, unless I can get someone to buy me
another. This is very possible. I'm muscular and hairy, with the
face of a back alley thug, perfect fodder for all those guys out there
with fantasies of getting it on with a knuckle-dragger. And they
are out there. I found out long ago that by just leaning against a
wall and looking stupid, I can usually draw in someone looking
for a little walk on the wild side.

Within half an hour I've hooked up with a couple of old
boyfriends with a place in the Village. One's a humpy little dago
with a tight compact body and dark soulful eyes. He tells me his
name is Lou, short for Luigi. His buddy is lighter, with blonde
hair, a kid's face, and the tall, lean body of a competitive swimmer. They both fall into the "sex candy" category, and I'm quite
happy to be their stray mutt for the night. We talk the usual bar-
room bullshit, and I answer their questions as politely as I'm capa-
ble of, waiting for them to make up their minds. When the blonde
guy, whose name is Charley, asks me what I do for a living, I tell
him I'm an iron man. Well, that tips the scales in my balance fast

enough; I can see they're about creaming in their jeans at the thought of making it with a *construction worker*. They exchange glances, raise their eyebrows and give each other a silent nod, with all the subtlety of a two-by-four between the eyes. It's funny, but they seem to think I'm too clueless to notice any of this. Or else they just don't care. They finally ask if I want to go home with them and I say "sure."

Riding in their car, I pick up signals that these guys want someone mean and stupid. I think about calling this off, but decide to just go ahead and play the game. When we get back to their place, I throw them around the bedroom, rough them up a bit, rip their clothes off, and then make them strip me naked. Lou pulls my pants down; when my dick springs out to full attention he looks like a kid who just got a new bike for Christmas. I grab his head and start fucking his face hard while Charley eats out my ass. Lou is no slouch at giving head. I close my eyes and let the sensations sweep over me of having my dick *finally* in some place warm and wet. We play out all the expected riffs on the theme of the big, bad construction worker. I call them "faggots" and "cocksuckers" and knock them around some more. But later on, I let them turn the tables on me. Charley "pins" me down as Lou slowly works a greased dildo up my ass. I snarl and spit, cursing threats at them, with all of us just having a grand old time. I end up fucking them both in retaliation, first Lou, then Charley, then Lou again, because I find him the hotter of the two. I shoot my load while plowing him, and as I squirt it deep into the condom up his ass, I throw back my head and bellow like a bull. A neighbor pounds on the wall and shouts at us to shut the fuck up. I lay back while Lou and Charley kneel over me and shoot on my face. They beg me to spend the night, but I tell them no, I got plans tomorrow morning. When they don't give it up, I kick over an end table and tell them to go fuck themselves. They love it.

On the subway back I think about how easy it was to give them what they wanted. Hell, if things get desperate enough, I could always try hustling. Christ, I hope it don't come to that.

I luck out. The next morning I finally land a job up on Lexington Avenue. One of the iron men there took a flop yesterday and fell two stories, breaking his leg. Tough luck for him. Lucky break for me. Oh, does that sound callous? Excuse me, I'll be more sensitive when I have more than fifty-seven bucks in my checking account.

I show up the next day right at eight o'clock, like I was told to; I'm not about to do anything to blow this gig. The building's a big motherfucker all right, already fifty-four stories worth of iron thrown up, with another twenty-two to go. I take the lift up to where the crew is punching in. By force of habit, I zero in on the humpiest guy there, some Irish piece of tail with a red crewcut, alert blue eyes, and a tight, sexy body that's just screaming for a serious plowing. I ask him what the foreman's name is and where I can find him.

He gives me a quick look over. "His name's Jackson," he says. "Last I saw him, he was over by the derrick bullwheel."

"What does he look like?"

He gives a hint of a smile. "Think pit bull on steroids." He buckles on his tool belt and hoists a coil of cable on his shoulder. "Just go over there. You can't miss him."

It don't take long to find Jackson. The guy was right. He does have the small blood-shot eyes and sloped head of an attack dog. I report in, and he looks me over, his eyes pausing for a second on the four gold rings in my left ear. He don't look too happy with what the cat drug in. We're standing just a few feet away from the bullwheel and have to shout to hear each other. "The hall tells me you're a connector," he growls. "Is that for real?"

I nod. "For five years. Out in L.A."

Jackson squints his eyes, a third rate Clint Eastwood. "Oh, yeah? Why'd you come out here?"

What, I think. *I need a passport?* But I know how crews guard their turfs like junk yard dogs. I give my best shit-eating smile. "Construction's gone to hell out West. All the trades are scrambling for work. I thought I'd try East for a change."

Jackson's squint don't lighten up any. Then again, maybe that's how he always looks. He points up to a figure balanced on an eight inch beam overhead, guiding down a twenty-foot I-beam hung from a derrick cable. Even from this distance I can see that it's the red-headed guy I talked to earlier. "That's Mike O'Reilly. You're going to be working with him bolting those headers." I start climbing up the column next to Mike's, but Jackson grabs me by the arm and pulls me back. By instinct my hand clenches into a fist, and I unclench it just as quick. I don't think slugging the boss would be such a good idea. "I'll be keeping my eye on you," he says, giving me the fisheye. "If you can't cut it, your ass will be off the crew by tomorrow."

Thanks for the pep talk, I think. I shimmy up the column with my eyes trained on Mike. He's perched on the beam, wrestling a header into place. I take a few seconds to take in the sight: his shirt off, his body packed with muscles, his powerful arms lifted up and struggling with all that steel against the backdrop of clear blue sky. Pure poetry. Enough to set my dick thumping. God, I love construction!

Mike is still humping the header when I finally get level with him, though with twenty feet of empty air still between us. "Howdy!" I call out to him.

He glances my way and then back at the header. He gives it a mighty whack with his spud wrench and then looks back at me again, his gaze bold as brass. His mouth curls up into an easy smile. "I wondered if you were Pete's replacement. How ya doing? Did Jackson chew a chunk out of your ass?"

"I still got most of it left." I grabbed my end of the header. "You need some help with that?"

"Yeah, if you feel so inclined."

I get the header lined up just so, slip a few bolts in, and tighten the nuts. I glance over to Mike. "You secure?" I call out. He nods. I hoist myself up onto the beam, trot out to the center and cut the choker loose. A gust of wind blasts me and I sway to compensate, nothing to fall back on but empty air. Girder surfing, we call it back in L.A. The building foundation pit is a tiny patch of blackness fifty-four stories below. Far enough down that if I took a dive, parts of me would splatter into Brooklyn. This don't bother me any. If it did, I'd be selling shoes for a living.

Mike and I pace ourselves like dancers, matching our rhythms and moves as we line up the headers and start bolting them down. I can see Mike knows what he's doing. He works the iron good, moving the beams easily where he wants them, and bolting them down quick and skillful. It don't take long before we get a heat up good and are snapping those beams into the columns like they're from a kid's erector set.

I find myself sneaking glances at Mike from time to time. He isn't exactly cocky, but he handles himself like a man who knows he's good and just lets his body take over and do what has to be done. It's late in the morning, now, and the sun is getting hot. Streams of sweat trickle down his torso, making it fuckin' *gleam*; drops of it bead around his nipples, which are as big as quarters and the color of old pennies. I think about what it'd be like chewing on them, flicking them with my tongue, nipping them with my teeth as Mike's muscular body squirms under me. His torso is nut brown but when he leans down to spin in a low bolt, I see his tan line and strip of creamy skin beneath it. His ass must be a very pretty thing, pale and smooth like polished ivory. Last night's fun and games haven't taken the edge off my hunger; if anything I'm stoked for more of the same.

We're on our fifth header by the time the lunch whistle blows. Mike pulls off his hardhat and wipes his forehead with the back of his hand; I watch as his biceps bulge up and dance. He stands there for a few seconds, his left knee bent, his weight on his right hip, that muscle-packed torso so nicely slicked. I feel my throat squeeze tight just looking at him. He's a slab of prime beef, all right, and my brain goes overtime thinking of all the dirty things I'd like to do to him. He suddenly turns and looks at me, and there's this second when my face is still naked, my thoughts written on it for anyone to see. I couldn't have been more obvious if I'd reached out and grabbed his basket. Mike's eyes burn into me and it's clear he *knows* what's on my mind. But he turns his head and gazes out towards the Jersey shore, like he's searching for something. Slowly, carelessly, he reaches up and scratches his balls, giving them a little extra tug. The signal is so fuckin' blatant that my brain buzzes with confusion. I'm surprised smoke isn't coming out of my ears.

Mike and I eat lunch together sitting on a girder with our legs dangling over 800 feet of nothing. Mike is relaxed and friendly, so open and at ease that I begin to wonder if I misread what was going on between us just a few minutes ago. I ask Mike how Pete, the guy whose place I'm taking, happened to fall.

Mike shrugged. "We were working a little late. I guess he was tired and just got sloppy. It happens."

After a while we run out of conversation. I lay on my back and close my eyes, feeling the sun beat down on me. I think about what

Mike looks like naked, and I give him a dick that's meaty and thick, just to keep the fantasy interesting. In my mind, he's fucking my mouth, slow and easy, his balls slapping against my chin. My dick gives a hard thrust against my jeans, but I don't do nothing to hide it.

"Thinking about pussy?" Mike asks. I half open my eyes and see him looking down at me, grinning. "I was just wondering. It looks like your dick's about to split your pants open."

"It's been a problem lately," I say, keeping my voice casual. "I seem to be horny all the time."

Mike's grin widens. "Well, maybe you'll get lucky soon." He winks his eye at me, and again I get that weird feeling he's sending me some kind of message. He stands up and dusts himself off. "Time to get back to work."

For the rest of the afternoon it's like that, Mike joking around, giving me these looks that may mean something, but then again maybe not. He's got me wound tighter than a clock, and I don't like it. For one thing, it's affecting my work now. A couple of times I fumble the bolts, stupidly watching them slip between my fingers and drop down all that space beneath us. I almost lose my spud wrench the same way, just grabbing it in the last half second before it's gone for good. I glance towards Mike, and he's watching me, grinning. "Uh, oh," he says. "You almost killed a businessman that time." His smile is good-natured enough, but his eyes gleam with a bold light that misses nothing. He's just having a good ol' time at my expense. I feel like pushing him off his beam.

At 4:45 Jackson signals for us to start wrapping it up. Mike cups his mouth with his hands. "Send another beam up!" he shouts. Jackson shakes his head and points to his watch. "We can do it!" Mike shouts back. "Al and I don't mind working a little late." Jackson shrugs and signals for the crane operator to hoist another beam up.

I glare at Mike. "What the hell's got into you?" I call over to him. "I want to go home."

Mike just grins. "The way you been fucking up this afternoon, I figure you owe the company a few minutes extra work." The beam swings down overhead, and he guides it into place. Pissed, I help line up the holes and slide a few bolts in. By the time he cuts the choker loose, the rest of the crew has taken off, leaving us alone. I spend a few more minutes bent over my end of the beam, slipping in the remaining bolts and tightening the nuts. I'm working as fast as I can so that I can just get the hell out of here and put an end to this day. I turn to see how Mike's doing with his end. He's still out there on the middle of the beam, only now his pants are down among his ankles. He's slowly stroking his stiff cock, his face as calm as if this is the most natural thing he could be doing. I almost drop my wrench for the second time that day.

"You ought to tie that thing around your wrist," Mike says, "before you kill someone."

I just stare at him. "What the fuck are you doing?"

Mike laughs. "What does it look like?"

I watch his hand slide up and down his thick dick, his balls bouncing heavily with each stroke. My own dick starts beating against my zipper, yelling to be let out. "Come on down to where there's some floor beneath us," I say. My throat's so tight I can barely get the words out.

Mike shakes his head. "No. I got a better idea. Come up here and join me."

The beam he's standing on juts out over the side of the building. I look down at the fifty-four stories worth of empty air beneath us. If we fell, I just might be able to shoot a load before hitting bottom, but there'd be hell to pay afterwards. I shake my head. "No way, Mike. I only practice safe sex."

But Mike just stands there grinning, his hand moving up and down his uncut dick. He stops for a minute and peels off his T-shirt. His sweaty torso gleams in the late afternoon sun, cut and chiseled in such a way that every muscle stands out. He tosses the shirt into the wind, and I watch as it floats down into oblivion. The street below is deep in the shadow of early evening, but up here it's still bright day. I spend a couple of seconds watching Mike standing there buck naked except for his hard hat, and I know I'm going to get it on with him or die trying. I jump up on the beam.

"Hold on," Mike calls out. "I want you to get naked first."

What the hell, I shrug. I'm ready for anything now. I do a careful strip, draping my clothes over the column head. Seconds later I'm bare-ass naked. A slight breeze plays over my body and I can feel the last rays of the sun on my skin. The steel's cool and smooth under my bare feet; everything else around me feels like miles of empty air.

Mike's lips curl up into a slow smile. "You look fuckin' great, Al," he says. He kicks off his shoes, and I watch as they disappear into the darkness below. He steps out of his pants, leaving them piled on the girder behind him. He's pumping his dick faster now, and I watch as his cockhead winks in and out of its foreskin. It makes for a great show.

I walk across the girder towards him like a man crossing pond ice on a sunny day. I've been walking for years on narrow beams above open space, and I feel my body automatically make the tiny adjustments that keep me from losing my balance. When I reach Mike I run my hands over his chest and torso, as much to steady myself as to feel his naked body. He leans forward and kisses me lightly, then not so lightly. We play duelling tongues for a while, and then Mike reaches down and wraps his palm around my dick. He glances at it and then back at me. "Jeez, you got a beautiful dick, Al."

"Yeah, I get a lot of compliments on it."

Mike grins. "I bet. Look how thick it is. And long, too. And how big and red the cockhead is." He laughs. "Not many men have a dick this pretty, Al. I hope you appreciate what you got." He squeezes my dick and a drop of pre-cum oozes out. He smears it between his thumb and forefinger thoughtfully. "Your balls have a nice size to them too, even though they're pulled up a little tight."

I give a stiff smile. "Being scared shitless has a way of doing that to me, Mike. Maybe we should just skip the commentary and move on to what's next."

Mike looks amused. He carefully bends down and picks up his jeans. He pulls a condom out of the back pocket. "All right, let's get to it. How 'bout plugging my butt hard."

I have to laugh. "Well, I'm glad you practice safe sex." None of this seems real. My cock is granite hard and I've never felt hornier. Mike spits in his hand and strokes my cock, making it slick. He slips the condom on over it and carefully turns around. I take his cue and with killing slowness impale his sweet ass.

I have never fucked with such concentration before. My mind is alert to every movement we make and my body is as tuned as if each nerve ending has a mind of its own. I begin pumping my hips, first with a slow, grinding tempo, then faster and deeper.

Everything is reduced down to one word: balance. Mike knows this too and he meets me stroke for stroke, his body reacting to the thrusts and pulls of mine like we're both well-oiled parts of one moving machine. I hold on to his torso, not roughly, but with a touch light and cautious enough to just barely feel the squirm of his muscles beneath my fingertips. We fuck like we're defusing a bomb, in carefully controlled terror. I have never had sex feel so goddamn exciting.

I spit in my hand and begin stroking Mike's cock. It's already slippery with pre-cum, and it slides easily in and out of my palm. Mike groans loudly and squirms against me, a move I wasn't expecting. For a second we sway to one side and I feel the beam slip from under my feet. Mike and I both quickly shift our weight and regain our balance. "Sweet Jesus," I mutter. But I never miss a stroke.

The lights are beginning to turn on in the buildings below us. The city spreads out beneath us to the horizon and I feel like I'm fuckin' flying. Even this far up I can still faintly hear the sounds of traffic from below. I plunge deep into Mike's ass and just leave my dick there, slowly rotating my hips. Mike groans again, this time louder. His dick in my hand is as hard as rebar, and I know it won't be long before it's ready to spew. I pull out almost all the way and then shove my dick hard back in again, till my balls press tight against Mike's ass. He cries out and I feel his spunk gush between my fingers and drip down into the darkness below. I hold on tight as his body shudders in my arms, keeping the control and balance for both of us. When he quiets down, I give my hips a few quick thrusts. That's all I need to get me off, and I feel my load shoot out into the condom up Mike's ass. I ride the orgasm out like a surfer on a killer wave, getting off on the thrill but concentrating on my balance all at the same time.

When the last shudder is over, I carefully pull out. Mike turns around and we kiss each other lightly, our bodies pressed tightly together. Mike makes a sudden jerking movement to the side and I feel a half-second of pure terror before I regain my balance. Mike laughs.

I glare at him. "You dickhead."

But Mike just keeps on grinning. He picks up his pants. "Come on, let's get off this damn beam."

Back by the foreman's shack, I give Mike my undershirt to replace the one he tossed over the side. But he's going to have to take the subway home barefooted. He just shrugs this off. As I get dressed I start thinking about what a fuckin' insane thing it was we just did. To my annoyance, my hands begin to tremble as I tie my shoes. I make sure Mike don't see this.

I look up at him. "Did you ever do anything this crazy before?"

The muscles in Mike's face twitch, like he's trying to decide whether or not to say something. Finally he gives a slow, easy smile. "Sure. How do you think the guy you replaced—Pete—fell?" He sees the expression in my face and laughs. "Hey, I was *joking*, okay? I've never done this before."

We ride down in the lift in silence. Mike is idly looking out towards the city skyline. I stare at his face, trying to figure out just exactly how Pete did fall off that girder.

Down on the street, Mike kisses me lightly. "See you tomorrow, Al. You're great working with." I watch as he walks barefoot down the sidewalk to the subway station on the corner, his arms swinging jauntily by his side. I shake my head. Jamming my hands in my jeans pockets, I plow through the crowds of people. When I get to the first street corner, I wait for the light to turn green, looking both ways carefully before crossing.

MUSCULAR MAYAN ADONIS

I'M STANDING IN the doorway of my cinderblock bungalow, looking out at the Gulf of Mexico. The sun hasn't cleared the mountains behind the resort yet, and the palms that border the beach are still in shadow. Out in the distance, however, the water is as shiny and flat as sheet metal. There's a faint breeze blowing in from the Gulf, bringing with it the smell of salt and seaweed, and a tropical warmth. In a few hours, it's going to be scorching, like it was yesterday, the day before, and in fact, the whole past week that I've been here. Since I have the metabolism of a lizard and have never met a day that I thought was too hot, this suits me fine.

I hear stirring behind me, and I turn and look inside. The window shutters are closed, and I can just make out in the dim light the outline of a human form, tangled up in the bedsheets. I wrack my brain trying to remember his name. Roberto? Alberto? Gilberto? It's useless, and I hope I can get away with just calling him "Berto."

Berto stirs again and stretches. "Hola, Juan!" he says in a sleepy voice.

"Hola, Berto," I reply. I walk across the room to the window and open the shutters. Light streams in, and I look at Berto's naked body. He squints and raises his hand to shield his eyes, letting loose with a torrent of Spanish. I smile apologetically and shrug. Berto grins back, flashing white teeth. He's very handsome, with his dark eyes and generous mouth and tight, sexy body, and the lust I felt last night sweeps over me again. Berto reminds me of the spiced Mexican chocolate sold in the village stalls: sweet, dark, and hot to the taste. He makes a gesture for me to approach and I'm only too happy to oblige.

When I reach the bed, Berto pulls me down and kisses me, slipping his tongue into my mouth. I shift to a more comfortable position, sliding into the bed alongside him without breaking the kiss. I'm wearing just a bathrobe, and Berto wastes no time in undoing its sash and throwing the robe open. His hands are upon me immediately, sliding down my torso, squeezing my nipples, kneading the flesh that looks so pale under his dark fingers. I pull him to me in a giant hug; Berto is lithe and slender and he feels like a young otter wriggling in my embrace. We kiss again, my hard dick pushing against Berto's tight, smooth belly. I slide my hands down his back and cup his firm ass, giving it a playful squeeze.

Berto spits in his hand and starts stroking my dick. I shudder and groan loudly, the sound trailing off into a sigh. Berto looks immensely pleased at having produced this reaction. He bends down and takes my dick in his mouth, sliding his lips down the shaft as he twists his head from side to side. I watch in awe as his head bobs up and down between my thighs. *Where does a kid that young learn how to give such head?* I wonder in amazement. Berto must be only eighteen or nineteen, but he's doing things with his tongue and hands it took me well over a decade and a half to learn. Berto's mouth nibbles and licks my dick, his tongue laps along the shaft, or darts down to my balls, drawing me to the brink of shooting and then backing off with the skill of a virtuoso playing before a concert audience. All I can do is lie back and let my body be the instrument for this performance, helplessly groaning as Berto conjures up another sensation. I close my eyes and listen to the *swoosh* of the ceiling fan and the slurping of Berto's tongue. I begin pumping my hips, fucking Berto's face with a slow, lazy rhythm that matches the rise and fall of his head. Berto's finger probes against my asshole and then pushes on in full against my prostate. The groan I give off is both loud and heartfelt, and Berto looks over at my face and grins. When he finally decides it's time to take me over the edge (we both know that *he's* running this show), he places his finger between my balls and presses down hard. The pleasure I feel is sharp and overwhelming. I cry out, thrashing in the bed as I squirt my load into the warm, wet confines of his mouth. When I'm done and lying in the bed, panting, Berto bends over and kisses me again. I taste my own sperm as I push my tongue into his mouth.

Berto swings his leg around and straddles my chest. He drops his balls in my mouth, and I suck on them eagerly as he strokes his cock. It only takes a few quick strokes on his part before he shudders and starts groaning. His load splatters against my face, dripping down my cheeks and chin and into my open mouth. Berto licks my face as if it were an ice cream cone and then slides into the crook of my elbow. The two of us lie still in the tangle of sweat-dampened sheets, as the heat pours into the room like warm honey. I absently follow the play of dust motes in the sunbeam streaming through the open window, feeling lazy and happy, like some big dog stretched out in front of a fire.

We eventually get up and dress, and I pay Berto the price we negotiated last night by the pier. I throw in an additional 50 pesos as a tip. Berto smiles and says something incomprehensible to me in Spanish, his eyebrows raised expectantly. I can only guess that he's asking if there will ever be a repeat performance. I give a friendly smile and non-committal shrug, while ushering Berto out the door.

Later that morning I think about Berto while I have my regular breakfast of Dos Equis and *huevos rancheros* at the village cafe I've been frequenting. I wonder if I should have gone ahead and arranged something for tonight after all. God knows, he's a firecracker in bed, and it's been a long time since I've had sex that good. I'm just not in a plan-making frame of mind right now. I stretch out my legs and gaze at a flock of pelicans skimming over the Gulf, smoking the one cigarette that I ration out for myself each morning. When I finish it, I dip into my afternoon ration and smoke another one. Eventually my food comes, which I eat with lazy gusto.

After breakfast, I wander down the streets of the small village, like I've done every day since my arrival. I'm getting to know this part of town very well: its cinder block buildings painted in pastel colors, its dusty roads, the limp acacia trees that ring the village square. The stroll is just something to do until I return to the resort and spend the rest of my day in a hammock reading one of my books and sipping beer. Usually, once I circle the square, I head back to my bungalow. This time, on impulse, I wander down a narrow alley that flanks the adobe church on the north end of the plaza. There's nothing much to see, just private residences with laundry strung out across the alley, and more children playing in the dust. I'm about to turn around when something catches my eye, a whitewashed store with the word *Souvenirs* printed in flaking red paint above the door. Conch shells flank each side of the concrete path to the door, so faded now from God only knows how many years in the sun, that their interiors have only the faintest tinge of their original pink. I decide to check the place out.

I push open the front door and a bell tinkles overhead. There's no one in the store, not even a proprietor behind the counter. I look around, squinting my eyes as they adjust to the dim light. The shelf that runs down the middle of the store is crammed with the typical tourist schlock: ashtrays, paperweights, pens, keychains, plastic dolls, all emblazoned with the word *Cozumel*. T-shirts hang on the wall, and they too have *Cozumel* printed on them beneath line drawings of sail boats skimming across stylized waves. Everything is covered with dust, and the shirts that are exposed to the sun's rays from the small window are as faded as the conch shells out front. It looks like nothing's been sold here in years.

I'm about to turn and leave when the curtains hanging from a door behind the counter part and a man enters the room. "Hola," he says smiling.

It's his smile that keeps me put; there's a warmth to it that is incredibly attractive. I smile in return. "Hola," I say.

"Americano?" the man asks. I nod. "Are you looking for something to take home with you?" he asks in heavily accented English. "Some kind of souvenir?"

"Maybe," I say, shrugging. I try to be subtle as my eyes sweep over him. He has a face that is truly arresting: the features mobile, the mouth wide and full, the high cheekbones, suggesting Indian blood. There is something wrong with one of his eyes, it stays fixed and half-lidded as the other follows me around. He seems to be about my age, early thirties, and he has a powerful build: broad shoulders, a muscular neck, and hands that are large and strong. Yet there's an air about him that is both dignified and gentle, maybe even melancholy, in the way he looks at me as we speak.

I look around for something I might buy. I half-heartedly pick up a porcelain ashtray shaped like a palm tree. It has "Welcome to Cozumel" printed in neat script along the length of the trunk. The proprietor shakes his head and smiles. "Perhaps the señor would be interested in a shell?" he says. He indicates a counter in the back of the room that I hadn't noticed before. I walk over and see through the glass a wild profusion of shells; they look like piles of hard candy: shiny, colorful, twisted into swirls, helixes, spikey cones. Most of them are small, the size of pebbles, but there is one larger one, about two feet long, mottled with black and tawny spots and ending in a sharp spire.

"What is that?" I ask, pointing to it.

The proprietor grins. "That is a *caracol*. I do not know the English word for it." He takes it out of the case and runs his fingers over it lovingly, a gesture surprisingly fluid given the strength and size of his hands. "I found it while diving off the reef on the south side of the island. That's where I find most of my shells." He hands it to me to inspect.

I feel the smoothness of the shell. "It's beautiful," I say softly. "How much is it?"

The proprietor laughs. "I would never sell it; it brings me luck." He takes the shell back and returns it to the case. He picks up a small, blue and gold snail's shell. "This is another one of my favorites." He drops it in my palm. "This one you can have."

I follow the gold threads of the spiral. "It's wonderful," I say. I put it in my pocket and pull out my wallet.

But the proprietor shakes his head and smiles. His teeth are white and even, and gleam in his dark face. He has a type of masculinity that I love: strong and calm and open. "It's a gift. Maybe the next time you come here I'll sell you something."

I find myself wondering what it would feel like to be in bed naked with this guy, our bodies pressed together. "My name is John Cutter," I say impulsively. I extend my hand.

The proprietor wraps his hand around mine but doesn't shake it. "Miguel Hernandez," he says. He holds my hand in his firm grasp long enough that I feel both confused and aroused. "Maybe I'll see you in my shop again, *Juan*. Or perhaps on one of the beaches on the south side of Cozumel. That's where I hunt for shells." He pauses. "That's what I'll be doing *mañana*." I wonder if I'm reading an invitation in Miguel's good eye or merely imagining it. Miguel releases my hand.

I leave the shop sporting a major hard-on, and for the rest of the day I feel restless and aroused. That night I look for Berto by the fishing pier, but without any success. I'm annoyed that I didn't arrange another visit with him. But when I finally go to bed, listening to the blades of the ceiling fan cut through the stagnant air, it's Miguel's face I conjure up.

The next day I rent a moped and drive across the island to the south side. I tell myself it's just to do a little sightseeing, that there's no hidden agenda involved here. But I'm careful to pack a couple of condoms and a container of lube in my knapsack. The road that cuts across Cozumel is as straight as a carpenter's plumb and ends in an abrupt T at the northern shore. The fork to the right is paved and reasonably well maintained. The road left is packed dirt and sand. I turn left.

The road deteriorates rapidly, and after about a mile, it just gives up and dies, fanning out into a flat bed of sand. Another moped stands parked along the side. Although it could be anybody's, I feel a small jolt of excitement. A dune runs to my left, blocking out the view of the Gulf, and I struggle up it.

The view that greets me from the top of the dune is incredible: white, fine grained sand stretching out in a broad swath in either direction for as far as the eye can see. The water close to shore is pure turquoise, gradually deepening to dark blue. I spot a towel a short distance away on the beach, with a pile of clothing next to it, but other than this, there's no sign of a human presence. The clothing and towel could be Miguel's; they could belong to somebody else entirely. I stake out my own territory a respectable distance away and unfold my towel. I strip down to my Speedos, slather myself with sun-block and stretch out on the towel. It's late morning, and the sun blasts the beach with enough heat to strain even *my* tolerance. I close my eyes and listen to the sound of the surf.

I'm halfway to drifting off when I feel a shadow across my face. I open my eyes and see Miguel standing over me, lined by the sun's rays. Except for a snorkel and face mask pushed over his forehead, he's naked. He's carrying his shell bag in his left hand and his skin glistens with beads of water.

"Hola, Juan," he says, grinning. "So we meet again!"

I sit up, squinting at him. With the sun behind him, he's little more than a silhouette of broad shoulders and muscular legs. "Hola, Miguel," I say, returning his smile. "I was hoping I'd run into you out here."

Miguel circles around to the other side of my towel. Now the sun is full on him, and I can see his body clearly. His skin is smooth, his torso powerful and solid, like seasoned oak. I trace a drop of water sliding down between the cut of his pectorals and across his hard belly. It disappears into his crisp black pubes. His dick flops against his right thigh, snakey, veined, with a dark, red-brown knob peeking out from the uncut foreskin. I feel my own dick stiffen, a fact not easy to hide when wearing only Speedos. I glance back up into Miguel's face and see him watching me closely with his one good eye. "Yes," he says calmly. "That's why I told you about this beach. As soon as I saw you in my shop, I could tell that we were *muy simpatico.*"

Miguel makes no effort to conceal the rush of blood to his dick as it lengthens and hardens. I sit still and drink him in with my eyes, tracing the lines of his body. The heat makes the air vibrate, and the dull roar of the surf takes on a hypnotic rhythm. The whole scene seems slightly unreal, something out of an old myth, some Mayan god rising from the sea. I reach up and wrap my hand around his calf, feeling the curve and hardness of the muscle. Miguel just stands there with his legs apart and his hands on his hips, watching me. My hand works its way up to his thigh, kneading the muscle, massaging it. His balls hang heavy in the heat, ripe and swollen. The back of my hand grazes against them, and I turn it over so that they rest in my palm. I roll them around in my hand, feeling their heft and texture, and then bend over and press my lips against them. The scrotal hairs tickle my mouth. I stick my tongue out and flick it against the meaty ballsac, bathing them with my saliva. I can taste the salt of the Gulf on them.

I wrap my hand around Miguel's dick, peeling the foreskin back from the dark cockhead. A drop of precum oozes out and glints in the sun. I bend over and lap it up, running my tongue over the fleshy, red knob and then slide my lips down the thick shaft. Miguel sighs loudly. I keep my nose buried against Miguel's pubes, savoring the sensation of my mouth full of his dick. With excruciating slowness, I slide my lips up his shaft, nibbling on it, tasting it, running my tongue over it. Miguel places his hands along either side of my head and begins pumping his hips. His dick slides in and out of my mouth, hard and urgent, and I twist my head from side to side to increase the sensation of my wet tongue against the meaty shaft.

Miguel pulls me to my feet and presses his body against mine. He hooks his thumbs under the elastic band of my Speedos and tugs them down. My dick springs to full attention, slapping against my belly. Miguel wraps his large hand around both our cocks, pressing them together, sliding the two shafts back and forth across each other. He bends over and kisses me lightly, his lips just a feather touch against mine. He does it again, and his mouth lingers long on mine before he breaks the contact. The next time, he plants his mouth firmly on mine, prying my teeth apart with his tongue, pushing it deep down my throat. We grind our hips together, our two dicks fucking his fist, our tongues wrapped around each other. I run my hands down his back, now slick with sweat, over the rise of his ass. I pry the cheeks apart, pushing my fingers into his crack, rubbing them against the pucker of his asshole.

Miguel lowers me down on top of the towel and stretches full length on top of me. He rotates his hips against mine, dry humping my belly. "Sit up on my chest," I growl.

Miguel grins. He swings his leg around and straddles my chest, his fleshy lowhangers swinging right above my mouth. I flick them with my tongue, then lick them long and hard, and finally suck them both into my mouth. Miguel slaps his hard dick against my face as I do this, rubbing it against my eyes, my nose, my cheeks. He shifts his weight until he sits full on my face. I burrow my face between his fleshy cheeks and tongue his asshole ferociously.

Miguel pivots around and deepthroats my dick, bobbing his head up and down as his lips slide along the shaft. His dick thrusts right above my face, and I take it in my mouth and suck on it hungrily. Miguel begins to tease me, mimicking every little sex trick I do to him. I roll my tongue around his cockhead, and he does the same to me. I nibble and chew on the dickshaft, and Miguel imitates me, nibble for nibble. I trail my tongue down below his balls and against his asshole, and soon I feel Miguel's tongue pushing against my own sphincter.

I come up for air and reach into my knapsack, pulling out a condom. "Miguel." I say, "I would really like to plow your ass. Is that okay by you?"

Miguel gives a quizzical smile. "Does 'plow' mean 'fuck'?" he asks.

"Yeah," I laugh. "Sorry, I don't know the Spanish word for it."

Miguel doesn't say anything. He takes the condom from me, tears open the package and unrolls it down my dick. He lifts his legs up, exposing the pucker of his asshole. I guess that's his way of saying "yes."

I take out the lube I brought with me and grease my dick thoroughly. I push my cockhead against Miguel's bunghole and then slide my cock on in. Miguel groans. "Slowly, slowly," he murmurs, and I stop and then inch my way in with killing patience. I pause while Miguel gets used to the idea of my dick up his ass. After a few seconds, I start pumping my hips, drawing my dick in and out of him with as much gentleness as I can manage. Miguel eases into the situation. I pick up the tempo, and Miguel matches me, thrusting his hips to meet me each time I plunge on in. Soon I'm plowing Miguel's ass like there's hell to pay, slamming into him with enough force to push him halfway into the sand.

Miguel's mouth is half-open, and little grunts come out of it with each inward thrust of my dick. He wraps his legs around my torso and with a sudden twist, flips me on my back. Now he's sitting on me, riding my dick, squirming on it, and it only takes us a second to match our tempos again. I reach up and squeeze his nipples hard, rubbing their nubs between my thumbs and forefingers. Miguel groans loudly and starts beating off. He bends his head down and we kiss, pushing our tongues together. The heat rises up from the sand and roasts my back while the noonday sun beats down on me from above. We're both drenched in sweat: it beads across Miguel's forehead, drips from his eyebrows onto my face and chest, streams down both our torsos. Our bodies slip and slide against each other like fat on a heated skillet.

I can feel my load being pulled up from my balls, and I give a long trailing groan. Miguel reaches behind and squeezes my balls, not gently. That's all it takes to push me over the edge. I cry out as I squirt my load up the condom in Miguel's ass, and he clamps his mouth over mine. We thrash around, Miguel riding me like we're in a rodeo, until my final spasm ends and I collapse in the sand. Miguel is furiously beating off. "When you shoot," I growl, "be sure to do it on my face."

"All right, then," Miguel gasps. "Here it comes!" He throws back his head and groans mightily as a ropy wad of jizz shoots out of his dick and splatters against my cheek. Another one follows, and then another until my face is caked with his cum. Miguel gives a final sigh and collapses on top of me.

We lie there like that on the beach, surrounded by a cocoon of heat. The surf pounding the sand is the only sound around us. After a few minutes we race out to the water and dive in, splashing each other like a couple of kids. We spend the day there, swimming and basking and when the sun finally squats upon the horizon like a fat, red hen, we stretch out on the cooling beach and fuck again.

That night I lie in my bed, holding the spiral shell that Miguel had given me. I keep turning it, tracing the gold thread that weaves across the dark blue background. The fan overhead pushes the hot air around uselessly, but I leave it on because I find the sound it makes soothing. I think about Berto and Miguel, wondering if they know each other, a high probability given the size of this village. *What would it be like,* I wonder, *to spend the night with both of them together?* My dick gives a throb just thinking about it, me plowing Miguel's ass as I deepthroat Berto. I close my eyes and drift off to sleep with that thought. Tomorrow I'll start seeing what it'll take to make it happen.

ECO SEX

Tony sits on my chest and drops his balls in my mouth. I reach up and twist his nipples as he slaps my face with his fat, red cock. My eyes drink up his body: the furred chest, the cut abs, the fleshy nipples that beg to be chewed, and, sweet Jesus, that face! Tony has a face that can stop traffic: dark, liquid eyes, a sensuous mouth, a rugged jawline. I stare at that face while I roll his balls around in my mouth and marvel again at what a fuckin' handsome man he is. I pour all my energies into just *being* here, noting every detail: the weight of Tony's body on my chest, the hardness of his thighs, the silky texture of his scrotum as my tongue works it over. It's going to be a long, dry spell for the next couple of years, and I'm going to need every hot memory I can rustle up for future jack-off fodder.

I glance at the clock on the bedstand. Hell, the airport shuttle will be here in half an hour! Much as I hate to, I'm going to have to speed this up. Tony catches my glance at the clock and nods. He takes his balls out of my mouth and replaces them with his dick, shifting his position to get a better angle at fucking my face. I reach up and squeeze his firm ass, feeling it clench and unclench as he pumps his hips. His dick is thick and meaty and fills my mouth. *Remember this!* I tell myself. *Get every detail stamped in your brain!* Tony is triggering my gag reflex and I struggle to take him all in. He sees my predicament and props my head up with the extra pillow. Yes, that's better. We settle into a steady rhythm, in and out, my hands holding his hips to support his weight, Tony's hands on the bed's headboard to steady himself. Sex with Tony is always athletic, and we're both working up a sweat. His torso gleams in the light from the early morning sun streaming through the window, and drops of perspiration bead his forehead.

Tony accompanies every thrust of his hips with a small grunt. The grunts are beginning to trail now, take on a higher pitch. I look up and see that his mouth is open, his eyes are glazing over. *It won't be long now*, I think. I start stroking my own dick as Tony continues to fuck my face. Tony groans loudly, and I reach up and press a finger tightly between his balls. Tony's body shudders violently and he cries out. He whips his dick out of my mouth just as his load squirts out, splattering me against my cheeks, my mouth, my eyes. I speed up the pace of my own strokes and it's only a matter of seconds before I shoot my load too, my spunk oozing out between my fingers. Tony leans down and kisses me hard, his tongue pushing deep inside my mouth as his dick had done a moment before. I pull him down and wrap my arms around him, feeling the tight press of his flesh against mine. *Remember what this feels like!* I tell myself.

Tony rolls over onto his back, and we lay flank to flank on the bed, staring up at the ceiling. I glance at the clock again. Twenty minutes until the shuttle arrives.

"I got to get ready," I say.

Tony shrugs but doesn't say anything. I jump out of bed and race into the bathroom. I look at the smears of Tony's load dripping down my face and grab a washcloth. But instead of wiping my face clean, I put the washcloth back in the rack, and rub the jizz into my skin. I want to feel Tony's load while I'm on the plane flying to Tucson. It'll be the last thing I'll have of him for a long, long time.

When I return to the bedroom, Tony is reaching for his jeans. "No," I say. "Stay naked. That's how I want to remember you."

Tony smiles and lies back on the bed, propped up on his elbows. His dick is softening now, but still half-hard. A drop of jizz dangles from its head. *What a beautiful man*, I think.

"You know, you don't have to go," he says. "You can still back out."

I shake my head. "It's too late. All the arrangements have been made." I start dressing. "Besides, I don't want to back out. Do you know how good it'll look on my resumé that I was a member of the Bioglobe team? Research labs will snap me up."

Tony frowns. "It's fuckin' crazy. Two years in a greenhouse with a bunch of whacked out scientists. You never even met these guys. They could be complete jerks."

I pull on my pants. Looking at Tony's naked body is getting my dick hard again, and I push it aside as I zip up. "A man's gotta do what a man's gotta do," I say, giving Tony my best John Wayne.

His mouth pulls down into something halfway between a grimace and a smile. I go to the mirror and comb my fingers through my hair. "So, any chance of you waiting for me?" I ask as casually as I can. "Two years isn't *that* long a time."

Tony gives me a classic poker face. "Which answer should I give, Tim? The one you want to hear or the truth?"

I turn around and flash Tony a big, phony smile. "Why, the truth, baby. As long as it's the answer I want to hear." A horn blast outside announces the shuttle's arrival, and I grab my bags. I glance over at the bed. Tony lies there with his hands behind his head, his left knee bent. I drink in his body with my eyes. "See you around," I say.

"Right," Tony says. He doesn't even try to sound convincing.

I'm a fuckin' idiot, I think, as I race down the stairs.

On the plane I close my eyes and wonder what I'm getting myself into. Tony's dried cum feels sticky on my face, but I make no effort to wash it off. I pull out from my briefcase the documents that Dr. Schiller sent me describing the project: the layout of the Bioglobe (the size of three football fields, containing six distinct ecosystems, all under 362,417 panes of glass) the six man team (one lead biologist—Dr. Schiller, one agricultural engineer, one botanist, one human behaviorist, one all-around handyman, and me, the bio-chemist, two months out of graduate school). I have never met any of these guys; all I've ever done is talk with Schiller on the phone a couple of times for the initial interviews. Tony's right, they could be complete buttheads. And I'm going to be stuck with them in a damn greenhouse for two years! On the phone I couldn't help but think that Schiller sounded like something of a cold fish, all business and scientific theory, his German accent giving his voice a clipped, humorless edge. I picture him as a tweedy sort, with his nose stuck in a textbook: coke-bottle glasses; thin, pursed lips; nervous, fussy mannerisms. *Knock it off*, I tell myself irritably. *You're just making things worse.* But I can't stop from trying to convince myself that I'm making a huge mistake.

When we land, I make a beeline to the baggage carrousel, where Schiller told me to meet him. I retrieve my luggage and scan the crowd for someone who conforms to my mental image. No one looks quite geeky enough. After a few minutes, I begin to get nervous. I don't know anyone in Tucson, and if I don't connect with

Schiller, I don't know where I'm going to stay.

A hand touches my shoulder lightly. "Tim?" a voice asks, and even in that one word I can detect the accent.

I whirl around. The man in front of me could pass for an Austrian ski instructor: a thick head of blonde hair, high cheekbones, and cool, blue eyes that regard me calmly. The body revealed under his T-shirt and cotton slacks is trim and athletic. "Dr. Schiller?" I ask incredulously.

Schiller flashes a smile that gleams in his tanned face. "Call me Otto. We're going to be living together for the next two years, so we might as well scrap all the formalities." He picks up one of my suitcases. "Here, let me help you. My car's parked outside."

Otto drives a beat-up Land Rover, covered with grit; the windshield is caked with grime except for the two half-moons cleared by the wipers. Driving to the Bioglobe site, he's warm and engaging. I smile to myself, thinking about how far off the beam my expectations were. It only takes a few minutes before we've passed through the Tucson strip malls and find ourselves out in high desert. The highway climbs up towards the approaching foothills, with a jagged line of mountains biting into the horizon ahead of us.

"Have the rest of the team arrived yet?" I ask.

"Yes," Otto replies. "You're the last. Everyone else has already set up camp within the Bioglobe. Tomorrow, we seal the doors shut and begin the great experiment to see if six humans can survive in a self-sustaining, artificial world for two years." He glances over towards me. "We don't have enough space for individual rooms, I'm afraid. I've got you bunking down with Buddy. He's the mechanic and all-around Mr. Fixit." Otto grins. "Buddy's a little wild, but I think you guys will hit it off." He reaches over and squeezes my thigh. "And if the accommodations don't work out, we can always change things around." Otto keeps his hand resting lightly on my thigh. I glance at it, tracing the tendons in the back of it, the long, strong fingers, the blonde hairs on his muscular forearm. I feel my dick begin to stiffen. Outside, the saguaro cacti and scrub brush whip by as we shoot up the flank of the nearest mountain.

We reach the gated road leading into the Bioglobe grounds just as the sun is settling down behind the mountains. The guard in the sentry hut smiles at Otto and waves us by. The road snakes up a small hill. We charge up to its crest and Otto slams on the brakes. My body jerks forward, and I brace my hand against the dashboard. "There she is," Otto says, grinning.

I look down into the narrow valley ahead of us, already half in darkness from the mountains' long shadows. "Jesus H. Christ," I murmur. Otto laughs. Bioglobe sits on a large clearing, still bright with sun. It looks like a giant ice castle, incongruously soaring above the Arizona desert. The last of the sun's rays sparkle off the glass panes, now turned rose. I can make out a mass of vegetation inside, pushing against the panes of the highest section.

"Over there," Otto says, pointing, "where all the vegetation is . . . that's the rainforest." His finger shifts as he speaks. "And the savannah is just to the right, with the swamp just below it. The desert is off in the western wing, by itself. You can't maintain a desert and a rainforest side by side. Too many contradictory demands on humidity control. The fields where we grow the grains are over next to the savannah. And there," his arm drops slightly, "at the lowest level, is our mini-ocean fully equipped with a coral reef and a wave-making machine." His arm arcs up again. "Living quarters are on the upper level, along with the lab and the communications control center." He bends down and turns the ignition on, and we descend down into the valley. Otto devotes all his attention to the bumpy road, as I stare out the window at the brightly glowing glass building. It looks like something out of *1001 Arabian Nights*.

When we pull up in front of the Bioglobe, Otto helps me unload my luggage. "I'm going to have to leave you here, Tim," he says apologetically. "There are still a million last minute details I have to take care of. Why don't you just settle in? Your room is on the top level, second door on the left." Before I can say anything, Otto has zoomed off into the desert night.

My room is simple but looks comfortable enough: a couple of beds, a few chairs, a table, some book shelves, a computer console. A Louis Lamour paperback lies face down on one of the beds, its title *Showdown at Dry Gulch* blazing in red across the front cover. There's a door, slightly ajar, next to the console. I hear the sound of running water coming from the other side. The sound stops. I push open the door, and see a young man, buck naked, standing on the bathroom floor, toweling himself dry.

He looks up at me unembarrassed. "Howdy," he says. "You must be Tim!" He drops the towel and holds out his hand. "I'm Buddy."

I shake his hand, forcing myself to keep my eyes from scanning down his body. The glimpse I caught when I first walked in was of muscle, tattoos, and thick dick meat. "Hi," I say.

Buddy flashes a boyish grin. His handshake is firm to the point of being painful, and I make a point of squeezing back with equal pressure. I try to break the contact but he holds on for a few seconds more before he releases my hand. I notice on his right bicep the tattoo of a bulldog's head, with *USMC* written above it. The left bicep has a snake curled around a bloody dagger. I take in the long hair, now plastered against his skull, the broken nose, the crooked front tooth, the shrewd eyes that don't miss a trick. He looks like a biker, and I find myself wondering how he's going to like being holed up in Bioglobe with a bunch of scientists. "I guess we're going to be roomies," he says. "You got any disgusting habits I should know about?"

"Not really," I say, smiling. "I'm pretty much of a regular guy."

Buddy's eyes scan me in frank appraisal. "Too bad," he says. "A little raunch ain't always bad." He picks up the towel and vigorously dries his back, his dick swinging back and forth heavily. When he's done, Buddy flips up the toilet seat and starts pissing in it. I watch the yellow torrent stream out. My initial impression was right; his dick is thick and meaty, a dark red shaft with a flaring head. I also notice how heavily his balls hang, the left one lower than the right, the scrotal sack loose and fleshy. "Hope you don't mind," Buddy says. "But I really had to go."

I pull my eyes up and meet his gaze; I can tell by the gleam in his eyes that he caught me staring at his dick. I can also see that he's pushing me, seeing how easily I get flustered. I step up to the toilet, unzip my fly, and pull out my own dick. "Mind if I join you?" I ask calmly. "It's been a long ride from the airport." My piss stream arcs down into the porcelain bowl, intercepting his. My dick is darker than Buddy's, uncut, maybe a little thicker, but it's hard to tell. Right now it's even money over who'd have the biggest hard-on. I wonder if we'll ever get a chance to find out.

Buddy grins, his eyes narrowing with amusement. He makes a point of shaking his dick more than necessary as the last drops of

piss trickle out. "I think we're going to get on just fine," he growls.
I smile back, feeling Tony's dried cum crinkle on my face.

It's the bees that bother me. Or rather the lack of them. After
three weeks in the Bioglobe, I hardly see them any more. We
started with a full swarm, the hive located in the thick of the rainforest, but today I've only counted a couple of dozen. Harrison,
the botanist, says that it's the glass panes of the Bioglobe; they filter
out the sun's ultraviolet radiation that the bees need to orient themselves and find their way back to the hive. None of us anticipated
this, and it is not good news. If we lose the swarm, we'll have to
cross-pollinate every friggin' plant by hand. I've made it part of
my daily routine to inventory the hive population, though when
I think about it, this seems like a rather pointless ritual. But it gives
me something to do.

The trail to the hive is a narrow boardwalk over muddy ground
and tangled roots. There's a small stream trickling alongside, one
of several dozen that lace through the forest. After a little while,
another stream joins it, and soon afterwards, another. I know
from previous explorations that there are a series of cascades further down that end in a waterfall emptying into a deep pool. The
hive is about thirty yards beyond that.

I turn the corner around a giant mango tree and see someone
standing in the pool under the cascading water. His head is
plunged into the waterfall, and all I can make out is a muscular,
tanned back and an ass you'd see on a piece of Greek sculpture:
smooth, dimpled, perfectly defined. The heavy drapery of leaves,
the green pool, the sound of the falling water, the slanting rays
from the desert sun all give the scene a nice exotic touch. The man
pulls his head out of the falling water and turns to me; I see that
it's Otto.

"Tim!" he exclaims, smiling. "How long have you been standing there?"

"Not long," I say. To my surprise, my heart is pounding. "Just
a few seconds." I shift my weight awkwardly to my other foot. "I
was going to check out the hive," I add. I feel like a Peeping Tom,
caught in the act.

"Why don't you join me?" Otto asks. "The hive can wait."

Otto doesn't have to ask me twice. It just takes a few seconds to shuck off my shorts and shoes and slip over the edge of the pool. The cool water slides over my body like an act of grace. "Sweet Jesus, that feels good!" I sigh. Otto grins but says nothing. I wonder if I should say something, ask Otto how he's enjoying the great Bioglobe experiment so far. But I don't want to break the mood with conversation. I close my eyes and settle deeper into the pool. *Fuckin' awesome*, I think. I hear the drone of a bee and remember the closeness of the hive. At least one of the poor bastards was able to find his way home.

Otto's foot brushes against mine. I wait for him to move it away, but instead it moves up my leg and begins rubbing against my calf. Startled, I open my eyes. Otto's blue gaze meets mine in unmistakable invitation. His smile is warm and lazy. "Come here, Tim," he says softly, and, with no thought or calculation I suddenly find myself pressed against him, my mouth fused over his, my tongue prying open his teeth and pushing its way deep inside. Otto's hands are all over me now, kneading the muscles of my torso, squeezing my ass, stroking the insides of my thighs. I wrap my arms tightly around his body and grind my hips against his, feeling his hard dick stab against my belly.

Otto breaks away for a moment and gazes at my face. "What a handsome boy you are, Tim," he murmurs. "I've wanted to do this ever since I first saw you in the airport." In my present state of horniness, I'm willing to forgive Otto for calling me a "boy." I pull him to me again and kiss him. Otto pivots us both around and suddenly we are under the waterfall, the water streaming down upon our heads and over our bodies. Otto reaches down and wraps his hand around my cock, stroking it slowly, running his thumb over the head. My body trembles, and he grins broadly. "Do you like that, Tim?" he croons.

"Yeah, Otto," I answer. "It feels fuckin' great." My hand finds his dick and returns the favor, stroking the skin over the head. I have still yet to *see* what his dick looks like, but I can feel its thickness, the solidity of flesh in my palm. The skin is loose, and, not surprisingly, given Otto's German origins, uncircumcised. I tug on his balls with my other hand and watch as Otto's eyes glaze over with pleasure.

There's a grassy spot alongside the pool, and Otto and I stretch out full length upon it. Otto lies on top of me, pumping his hips, dry humping my belly, as we play dueling tongues. He kisses me lightly on my eyes, my nose, my throat, and then sits up, his thighs straddling my chest. I reach up and twist his nipples, drinking in his body with my eyes: the broad chest lightly dusted with blonde hair; the wide, pink nipples; the tight belly. His cock juts out at full erection, the head flared and red, the foreskin peeled back, the bluish veins snaking their way up the shaft. I wrap my hand around it and squeeze, watching as a clear drop of pre-cum oozes out. I run my thumb over it, rubbing the sticky fluid between my fingers. My hand slides down around his balls and cups them. I look up at him. "You got a load in there for me, Otto? Something thick and juicy you can splatter against my face?"

Otto's blue eyes have lost their coolness, and I can clearly see the hunger in them now. I feel a little buzz of power and gently increase the pressure of my grip on his balls. Otto groans. "Yeah, Tim," he growls. "I got something for you, all right."

He thrusts his hips forward, and I open my mouth, letting his dick slide in. I seal my lips around it as it pushes to the back of my throat. *Jeez, is it good to have dick in my mouth again!* I think. I had thought that I was going to go without for two years. Otto pulls back, and I roll my tongue over his shaft as it withdraws, slurping on it noisily. He seizes my head with both hands and begins plowing my face with quick, vicious thrusts, each time pushing his dick deep enough down my throat to push my nose hard against his dark blonde pubes. I grab two handsful of asscheek and squeeze hard.

"Well, damn! Ain't that a pretty sight!" a voice booms over us.

I look up startled, trying to disentangle myself from Otto's body, almost falling back into the pool in the process. Buddy is standing over us, wearing nothing but shorts and sandals. A towel is draped over his shoulder. He's grinning, but his eyebrows are pulled down, and his eyes are fierce. I am totally thrown for a loop, but when I glance at Otto, he doesn't look particularly bothered. "Hello, Buddy," he says. "I'd just about given up on you."

"I was working on one of the heat pump motors," Buddy says. "It took longer than I thought it would." He talks in the matter-of-fact voice of someone making conversation over the dinner table. He nods towards me. "You sure as hell didn't waste any time finding a pinch hitter."

My gaze shifts from Otto to Buddy and back to Otto again. "Wait a second," I say. "You were expecting Buddy all along?"

Otto laughs. "Well, I wasn't sure. He was supposed to be here forty minutes ago." He glares at Buddy. "But Buddy isn't so reliable sometimes." He shrugs. "And then you came along and things worked out just fine."

Buddy's grin widens. "You gotta understand, Tim. Otto is one of the all time dick pigs." I blink, a little taken aback by Bioglobe's head scientist being called a "dick pig," but Otto laughs again, as if Buddy has just complimented him. Buddy's eyes dart back and forth between us. "Soooo, is this a private party? You guys want me to leave?" Buddy adopts an exaggerated pose of a forlorn little boy.

"Yeah," Otto says. "Beat it. We don't want any street trash around here."

Buddy looks at me with a deadpan expression. "You see how he talks to me!" He shakes his head. "No respect at all." His mouth curls up into a slow, sly grin, and he pulls down his zipper. "Just for that, fucker, you're going to have to wait your turn. I'm goin' to plow Tim's ass good and hard and make you watch." He steps out of his shorts and kicks them aside. His fat, red dick has swelled to half-hardness, and swings heavily between his legs. He glances at me. "That is, if you got no objections."

"I appreciate your asking," I say drily. My eyes scan over his muscled, tattooed body, his biker's attitude all the sexier for being so unposed, the thick cock rapidly hardening before my eyes. "Why don't you just get the fuck over here," I growl. "And let's get this party going."

Buddy laughs. "A man after my own heart!"

His half-hard dick sways heavily from side to side as he walks towards us, and I feel my mouth salivate. I open wide and take it all in, slurping noisily as Otto drops to his knees and tongues Buddy's balls. Buddy reaches down and lifts my chin, his dick still in my mouth. He gazes for a long moment into my eyes. "Do you have any idea," he growls, "how goddamn sexy it is to look down and see my dick being chowed down by such a hot fucker?" There's no response I can give to that except to keep on sucking.

Otto sits back on his haunches. "Did you bring the condoms?"

he asks.

"Hey," Buddy snorts. "Do I look fuckin' stupid?" He breaks free from my mouth, retrieves his shorts, and pulls out a small, tin-foil square. "All right, Tim," he grins. "Stand up and grab your ankles."

Buddy fucks like a steam driven piston, full of hard, grinding thrusts and lots of snorting and wheezing. His hands firmly grip my hips as he skewers me, and he handles the business of plow-ing my ass with the concentrated competence of a handyman who knows what he's doing. "How does that feel, you sexy bastard," he grunts. "How do you like having a man's thick dick up your ass?"

At the moment I can't answer him, because Otto's big dick is crammed deep down my throat. It probably was a rhetorical ques-tion anyway. Otto leans forward and slides his hands across my back, massaging the muscles. I gobble greedily on his meat, roll-ing it around with my tongue as I give his balls a series of firm tugs. I pump my dick with my other hand, stroking it in rhythm to Buddy's thrusts. I have never taken it from both ends before, and the sensation of being so full of *dick* is heady stuff. I'm getting drunk on dick, acting like a goddamn wild man. I twist my head from side to side and suck hungrily, feeding off Otto's meat as I clamp my ass muscles down hard on Buddy. Both men groan, and Buddy's hands slide over to my nipples, twisting them hard. "Another dick pig," Buddy growls, "feeding at the trough." Otto laughs.

Buddy shoves his dick all the way with a savage thrust and keeps it full up my ass, grinding his hips hard against me. *"Ride it, fucker!"* he shouts. Now it's my turn to groan. Buddy resumes pumping his hips back and forth with fast, deep strokes. "Every-body's got something to hide 'cept for me and my monkey!" he sings loudly, punctuating every downbeat with another hard thrust. *The guy's a lunatic!* I think, and the thought of being plowed by someone this crazy sets my dick throbbing. I spit in my hand and speed up my strokes, and my body trembles. *"Yeah,"* Buddy shouts. *"Get down! Get funky!"* Otto slaps his dick against my face, striking each cheek with a sharp *thwack!* and I start suck-ing on his balls. I look up at his face, his scrotum in my mouth;

Otto's eyes are wild, his mouth pulled back in a grimace. Sweat pours down his face and drips onto me in a steady stream. Above his head, a banana tree frond waves lazily from the breeze coming from one of the ventilating fans. And above that, the desert sun blazes down through the glass panes.

"Oh, shit, I'm going to shoot!" Buddy bellows out. He pulls out and rips the condom off. I roll over and watch as his fat dick pulses out one ropy strand of jizz after another, splattering against my face and chest. Buddy groans and wheezes with each throb of his dick. Then Otto starts groaning, and his load pulses out as well, squirting down on me, mingling all over my face with Buddy's jizz. "Fuckin' A!" Buddy croons.

Buddy sucks on my balls as I stroke my dick, and when I finally come, it's like being hit with a pile driver. I arch my back up and let 'er rip, spewing jizz into all directions, crying out like a howler monkey. Otto plants his mouth over mine and tongues me fiercely until the final tremor passes through my body, leaving me limp and exhausted. I lie there, eyes closed, panting, listening to the gurgle of the waterfall. "Jesus H. Christ!" I finally groan. "That one just about did me in!"

Otto laughs and Buddy stands above me, grinning, his dick still half hard, a last pearl of jizz hanging from the cumslit. He reaches down and pulls me to my feet. "Welcome to Bioglobe!" he says, his grin widening. "You've now been officially initiated!

We dress in silence, a silence that remains with us as we thread our way across the savannah back to the living quarters. Once there, Buddy and I share a shower together. "I thought my sex life for the next two years would consist of jerking off when nobody was looking," I tell Buddy, as I soap down his chest.

Buddy slides his hands over my ass and pulls me towards him. "Now that sure as hell would be a waste, wouldn't it?" His fingers pry apart the crack of my ass and massage my tender bunghole. "Believe me, little buddy," he growls in my ear, "sex is the one thing for sure you won't be short on. Ol' Otto and me will make a point of that!"

I wrap my arms around him, and our soapy bodies slide together under the spray of water.

CONVICT DICK

IT WAS ONE OF those August days where the heat just bore down on you like slow death. Nothing but burnt out corn fields to my right. Over on my left, a couple of fishing boats chugged down the brown sluggish waters of Hull Creek, heading out to the Chesapeake. No air conditioner in my old clunker; the only way to survive was to keep all the windows rolled down and pray for a breeze. As I cruised down the dirt road, my car kicked up clouds of fine, red dust that billowed inside and coated everything: the dashboard, the seats, the inside of the windshield. I could taste the grit in my mouth when I swallowed, good ol' red Virginia clay. Up ahead I could see the dark ribbon of Highway 17 cut perpendicular to the road I was on; asphalt never looked so good.

There was a road gang working on the highway. A beat-up old truck stood on the shoulder, two men standing on its bed and pouring hot asphalt down onto the roadway. Three other men were on the ground, raking the asphalt level. They all stood under the blazing sun, shirtless and sweating buckets, pushing that steaming tar around like they were the damned from hell and this was what they had to do to set things straight. Off to the side a couple of good ol' boys, foremen I guessed, stood quietly by, watching them. Their faces had all the expressiveness of two slabs of tenderloin.

I stopped at the intersection and watched the crew for a couple of seconds. It made me squirm just to think about what it must feel like out there on that hot tarmac. Fried beef. One of the men on the road straightened up and wiped his head with his forearm. Instinctively, I checked him out. He looked like the youngest guy there, mid-twenties, around my age. Sandy hair, streaked with dust, the high cheekbones and wide mouth of Appalachian white trash, and a tight, compact body packed with muscles and ready for trouble. Guided by some mountain hunter's instinct, he must have felt my eyes on him. He raised his head and looked directly at me; though his eyes were squinting in the sun, I could still see that they were as blue and hard as cool steel. Sweat trickled down his face in a steady stream.

I turned onto the highway and pulled alongside of him. Impulsively, I reached into my back pocket and pulled out my old bandanna. I handed it to him. "Here," I said. "You need this more than I do." Instead of reaching for it, he backed away. The two foremen stiffened and stepped forward. *What's this all about?* I wondered. "Hey, you!" one of the foremen yelled at me. I decided it would be a good idea to move on, and I pulled away fast.

Old man Edwards was holding his usual position behind the counter of the Kilmarnock Grocery Store. He grinned at me as he rang up my six-packs and groceries. "This heat done you in yet, Pete?" he asked.

I shrugged. "I'm taking it all in stride. In the evening the breeze comes in from over the creek and cools things down a bit." I gave a small laugh. "I hope the state is paying that road crew back there a hefty salary. That's sure shit work to do in this kind of heat."

Edwards snorted. "Hell, the state ain't paying those guys nothing but three squares a day. That's a prison gang, son. They're just serving time."

I stared at him. "You're kidding me!"

Edwards shook his head. "Hell, no. If it weren't for the prison labor, most of the roads back here would never've been built."

I considered this. "I thought prison gangs were kept in chains and the guards all carried shot guns."

Edwards laughed. "You been watching *Cool Hand Luke* too many times, Pete. It's not like they're letting murderers out on the crew. These guys are all just two-bit criminals."

I thought of ol' Sandy Hair. If he wasn't mean enough already going into prison, working out there on the hot asphalt all day would sure enough finish the job. I thanked Edwards and went on with my errands. By the time I was ready to head back, the sun was low down in the western sky. If the heat had slacked off any, I sure as hell couldn't tell.

The road crew was still at it, a couple of miles closer to town now. One of the lanes had a new layer of asphalt and was shut down to traffic. Sandy Hair waved me down and I braked to a halt. He came up to my car and leaned down.

"We're lettin' the cars from the other direction come through first," he said. "You're goin' to have to wait a couple of minutes." My initial hunch was right; his drawl was pure Appalachian. If he recognized me, he gave no indication. I looked over his shoulder. A Greyhound bus was inching down the one lane, between the traffic cones. Both guards were off with the other men, directing it through.

I turned back to Sandy Hair, but he wasn't looking at me. He was staring at the six-pack of Buds sticking out of the top of the grocery bag beside me. He was looking at them the way a Baptist would look at a piece of the True Cross. "You want one?" I asked.

His gaze shifted back to me, and he gave me a hard look, his blue eyes narrowing dangerously. *This is not a guy to fuck around with*, I thought. After a couple of beats, his mouth curled up into a slow grin. "Mister," he drawled. "I'd slit my grandma's throat for one, now." He glanced behind him. One of the guards was looking over at us. Sandy Hair straightened up. "But I better not. I could get into deep shit if I tried to sneak one." He stepped back as if to walk away, but before he did his eyes slid down my body in unmistakable appraisal. His glance met mine again and he winked. "Thanks for the offer, though. Both for the beer and the bandana." He turned and walked away. After a couple of minutes he waved me and the cars behind me through.

That night I laid in bed with not even a sheet over me. The heat pressed down on me like a flat iron on wrinkled cotton. The fan on the bedtable did nothing but push the hot air around a little, and my pillow was damp with my sweat. *Fuck it*, I thought. *There's no way I'm going to be able to sleep in this weather*. I got up, pulled my jeans on, and grabbed my flashlight. Sometimes, when it gets like this, I just lie down on the dock by the creek. It's cooler down there, and if there's a breeze anywhere around, it'll come from over the water.

The rough wood of the dock felt good under my back, and I just lay there quietly, looking up at the night sky. There was no moon out tonight and the stars blazed. The only sounds I could hear were the creek frogs croaking and the waves lapping against the pilings. I was just drifting off when I heard a loud *thunk* come from inside the boat house. Nothing in there but my beat up old motor boat and my fishing gear. Sometimes raccoons squeeze in through one of the loose boards and get into the bait bucket; the little bastards can make an unholy mess. I decided it was worth getting up to scare them off.

I sneaked up to the door, flung it open and shined my flashlight inside. There weren't any raccoons inside, but Sandy Hair was there, stretched out in my boat, his long legs dangling over the edge. He bolted up, squinting in the light's beam. I just about dropped my light in surprise.

"What the hell are you doing here!" I asked.

Sandy Hair said nothing. He just kept on squinting in my direction. After a while, he finally spoke. "Mister, would you mind not shining that goddamn light in my eyes?"

I shifted the light so that he was just caught in the edge of the beam. Neither of us said anything for a couple of seconds. It was pretty easy to figure out what happened. "You're on the run, aren't you?" I said. Sandy Hair didn't answer. He didn't have to. I thought about how I should play this. "Come on up to the house," I finally said.

"You got a gun?" Sandy Hair asked. It was clear that with the beam on him, he couldn't see who was talking to him.

I shook my head, a gesture wasted in the darkness. "No."

"Then why the hell should I do anything you tell me to?" he asked. His tone was more practical than belligerent.

"Because it's a hell of a lot more comfortable in my house than in my damn boat," I replied. I swung the light around so that my face was lit up. "Remember me? The guy who offered you the beer?" Sandy Hair's face was expressionless. There was another long pause. "Yeah," he drawled. "I remember you. You alone?"

I wondered how smart it would be to admit that. "Yeah," I finally said. "I'm alone. Are you coming?"

Sandy Hair just sat there, looking at me with narrowed eyes. He finally stood up, swaying to keep his balance in the rocking boat. He stepped out onto the planking that ran along the boat house wall. "Just lead the way."

"So what're you going to do?" Sandy Hair asked. He was sitting at the kitchen table, a chicken leg in one hand, a beer in the other. I shrugged. "Nothing. You can spend the night here, but

I want you out by tomorrow morning."

Sandy Hair looked at me speculatively. "How do I know you ain't goin' to call the sheriff as soon as I drop off?" He took a long swig from the can in his hand. "Maybe I should just tie you up."

I met his gaze. "You could try." Sandy Hair had bigger muscles than me, but I was taller and broader in the shoulders. I didn't know if I could take him on, but I figured I had at least a fighting chance. "Listen," I said. "I got no stake in turning you in. What you did is none of my business."

Sandy Hair stretched. "Then I guess I'll just have to trust you." The way he smiled made what he said seem like a joke. He finished off his beer, crushed the can and tossed it in the garbage. He looked at me. "You know what I want more than anything else right now? A bath. I stink like a damn pig, working out on that goddamn road gang all day."

"The bathroom's down the hall," I said.

His mouth curved up into a slow smile. "Don't mean to offend you, buddy, but I just as soon not leave you alone in the kitchen with the telephone." His grin widened. "I didn't say I had to trust you *completely*. Would you mind stayin' in the bathroom with me as I wash up?"

I looked at him stretched out on the chair, taking in the tight muscular body, the powerful arms, the unmistakable bulge in the prison-issued trousers. I felt my dick begin to stiffen. "Not at all," I said, keeping my voice calm and easy.

Steam rose up from the tub as it slowly filled. I sat on the closed toilet seat as Sandy Hair pulled off his shirt. Once more I got a chance to check out his fine, fine body, the torso packed tight with muscles, the skin gleaming with a light sheen of sweat. The nipples were nut-brown and wide, the size of quarters, and they begged me to chew on them. A light crop of brown hair dusted his pecs and trailed across his tight belly into the waistband of his pants. He was right about needing a bath. Even from where I sat, the smell of old sweat was pungent, almost rank. I closed my eyes and inhaled deeply.

Sandy Hair pulled down his pants and kicked them off; all he had on now were his frayed, prison-gray undershorts. His legs were long and muscular, good legs for outrunning prison guards. Something about the slow, deliberate way he was stripping made me wonder if he was testing me for my reaction.

"You've really kept yourself in shape," I said.

Sandy Hair looked pleased. "When those assholes don't have me out pushin' tar, I spend a lot of time in the prison yard, pumping iron." He pulled down his shorts and kicked them away. His dick was fat and meaty, uncut, the head peeking out from the dark foreskin. It flopped against his thigh in a way that made my throat tighten up. His balls hung low and heavy in the summer heat. Sandy Hair turned around and stuck his big toe in the water to test it. His assflesh was pale and creamy, a sharp contrast to his deeply tanned torso. It was an ass you could write poems about. My dick was as hard as a pile driver, and I just hoped my old jeans were baggy enough to hide that fact.

"What were you in for?" I asked. I was trying like hell to keep my tone of voice conversational.

Sandy Hair stepped into the tub and eased himself down. He closed his eyes and sighed. After a few seconds, he looked at me. "I knocked off a 7-11 over by Roanoke. It was my second offense, so they gave me five years. I have another eighteen months before I'll be up for parole."

I rolled this over in my mind. "What's your name?" I asked.

Sandy Hair lathered up. "Virgil." He grinned. "Pretty fuckin' stupid name, isn't it." I laughed. "What's yours?" "Pete," I said.

Virgil reached over and we shook hands. "Glad to know ya, Pete. You're a real friend in need." He waved his hand in a way that seemed to take in the whole house. "Must get pretty lonely out here, all by yourself."

"I get by," I said.

Neither of us spoke for a while. I watched Virgil soap up his pits with a twinge of disappointment. I would have loved to have buried my face in them and sniff them for days. He scrubbed his torso and arms, and lifted up his legs to scrub them too. I was getting so damn horny, I felt I could shoot a load right there. Finally, Virgil stood up, the water running down the length of his naked body.

"You got a towel I can use?" Virgil asked.

I reached over to the towel rack and tossed him one. Virgil began to dry his body vigorously. He put the towel behind his back and rubbed. I watched as his dick and balls swung heavily back and forth. When I looked up, my eyes met his. He smiled.

"You can suck it if you want to," he said amiably.

"Wh . . . what?" I stammered.

Virgil's expression was friendly. "I said you can suck my dick, if you want. God knows you been looking at it like you was a starving dog and it was a T-bone steak." He tossed the towel on the floor. "In fact, you'd be doin' me a favor if you did. It's been a helluva long time since I last got a blow job."

I didn't say anything for a while. There was no noise in the room except the gurgle of bathwater going down the drain. "It's been a long time for me, too," I finally said. "It's slim pickings around here for a guy like me."

Virgil's grin broadened. "Well, then, hot damn, Pete! Let's get down to it!"

That was all the invitation I needed. I dropped down on my knees in front of Virgil and took his dick in my mouth. I rolled my tongue over it, savoring the feel of another man's meat down my throat. I couldn't remember how long it'd been since I'd last tasted cock. Too damn long. It didn't take much work on my part to get Virgil's dickmeat to start stiffening. I felt it swell in my mouth, getting longer and thicker, the cockhead pushing against the back of my throat. Sort of like inflating a life raft inside your house; you didn't know if the room would be big enough for it to fit.

I made room. I began to slide my lips up and down the shaft, twisting my head from side to side. Virgil groaned. "Yeah, buddy," he crooned. "Work that dick." He began pumping his hips in time to my sucking. I reached back and cupped his ass, feeling the muscles tighten and relax with each thrust.

I pulled away and buried my face in his balls, inhaling deeply. Even after Virgil's bath, I could still faintly smell their musky odor. I took his ballsac in my hand and hefted it. His nuts hung low and heavy in my palm. I looked up at him and grinned. "Hell, they're a meal and a half all by themselves!"

Virgil laughed. "Well, then, chow down, Pete!"

I kissed his balls gently, pressing my lips against the loose flesh; the light scrotum hairs tickled the skin around my mouth. I opened my lips and sucked his balls in, teasing them with my tongue the way I had done his cock, seconds ago. I raised my eyes, my mouth full of scrotum meat. High above the expanse of tight, muscular flesh, Virgil's face loomed over me. "You having a good time?" he asked, his eyes mocking.

Before I could answer, Virgil hooked his hands under my armpits and tugged me to my feet. He pulled my face to his, and kissed me, slipping his tongue deep into my mouth. I folded my arms around his naked body and pressed him tightly against me. His torso squirmed against mine, and I felt his dick dry hump the front of my jeans. Virgil pulled back. "You know what your problem is, Pete?" he said. "You got too many damn clothes on."

I grinned. "Well, let me see if I can do something about that." I unzipped my fly.

Virgil stepped out of the tub. "You got a bedroom around here somewhere? Or do you just hang yourself in a closet at night?"

"Down the hall," I laughed. "Let me show you."

As I pulled off my pants, I watched Virgil lie stretched out on my bed, stroking his dick. "I been wanting to see you naked since I first spotted you on the road," he crooned.

I stood at the foot of the bed, hands on hips. "Well, you got your wish, Virgil," I grinned. "Now what?"

"Come over here and fuck my face," Virgil growled. "Nice and slow. Make it last."

I jumped onto the bed and straddled his torso. Holding his head with both hands, I slid my dick deep into his mouth. Virgil's tongue played over it like something with a life of its own. I began pumping my hips in rhythm to his sucking, closing my eyes as the sensations swept over me. I opened them again. I didn't want to miss the sight of my dick crammed into the mouth of this hot mountain man.

I took my cock out and dropped my balls into Virgil's mouth. He sucked on them eagerly as I slapped his face with my dickmeat. I spat in my hand and reached behind me, wrapping my palm around his dick. He thrust his hips up, and his thick dickmeat slid up and down inside my spit-slicked hand. He groaned, his voice muffled by a mouth full of scrotum.

Virgil wriggled farther under me until I was sitting directly on his face. His tongue squirmed between my ass cheeks and probed into my bunghole. His tongue licks were like electric jolts up my body, and I gasped for the sheer pleasure they gave me. I rolled off him. "I want you to fuck my ass," I growled.

Virgil looked up at me with a sly smile. "Anything to keep you from calling the sheriff, Pete."

I reached into my nightstand and pulled out a condom and jar of lube. Virgil laughed. "I thought you said you never get laid!"

I shook my head. "Not 'never.' Just not often enough."

I slid the condom down Virgil's dickmeat as he lubed up my ass. He threw me on my back and slung my legs over his shoulders. I felt his cockhead press against my bunghole, and then, with excruciating slowness, his dick slid up my ass. He skewered me good, thrusting deep inside of me, his balls pressed hard against my ass cheeks. He ground his hips in a circular motion, and it felt as if there were at least two feet of dick up my ass. I groaned.

"You gettin' your money's worth, Pete?" Virgil grunted. He started pumping his hips, driving his dick in and out in long, rapid strokes. I moved my body in rhythm to his, matching him thrust for thrust. I reached up and pinched his nipples, not gently. His eyes narrowed and a mean blue light came into them, but his mouth curled up into a lazy smile. "Yeah, that's good, buddy," he growled. "Play rough." He bent down and planted his mouth over mine, never missing a stroke.

I squeezed my legs around his torso and flipped him over. I rode his dick like he was a runaway train, working it with my ass, squirming on his torso. Virgil scooped a dollop of lube out of the jar and started jacking me off. Sweat dripped down from my forehead into my eyes and onto Virgil's chest. I could see Virgil was drenched too; our bodies were slippery with it. The heat made our fucking take on a slow-motion, dreamy quality, like fucking under water, like fucking in thick, hot mud. The only sounds in the room were our grunts and sighs and the steady slap of wet skin upon wet skin. I squeezed my ass muscles tight and then loosened them, as I slid up and down Virgil's fuckpole. It wasn't long before that cool, hard light in his eyes was gone, replaced by a feverish gleam. His mouth was half open, and he gasped in the humid air with a ragged breath just shy of a groan. I bent down and licked his nipples and this time he did groan, a long, trailing one that seemed to come from his gut. "Ah, baby, that feels so good!" he whispered.

I reached behind and cupped his balls in my hand. They had

pulled up and were tight against his body, ready to squirt. I gently squeezed them and Virgil shuddered. "Jeez, I'm about to shoot," he moaned. I pressed between his nuts, hard, and that pushed him over the edge. He cried out, arching his back, thrashing around in my bed like a bronco, and I just hung on for the ride. I felt his dick pulse inside me, squirting load after load of sweet jizz into the condom up my ass. His lube-smeared hand was still working my dick, and I could feel my own load rising out of my balls. I fucked his fist with a couple of long hard thrusts, and that was enough to do the trick. I threw back my head and hollered out. The first spurt of jizz hit Virgil just below his right eye. A second load came, then a third, until his face was dripping with my cum. A drop of it hung from his lower lip. I bent down and licked it off, and we kissed long and hard, our tongues pushing towards each other's throats.

I collapsed beside him. I meant to get up and get Virgil a towel to clean up with, but my body felt too heavy to move. We lay motionless in the sweat-soaked sheets, too exhausted to do anything but drift off to sleep. Once, I woke up briefly a couple of hours later. Virgil was snoring gently. By the light coming from the hall, I could still see smears of my cum on his face, mingled now with his sweat. I drifted back to sleep.

Virgil left the next morning, wearing some old clothes of mine and carrying with him thirty-seven dollars, all the money I had in my wallet. His escape was big news in the local papers for a couple of days, but after a while, when nobody found him, the story moved to the back pages and eventually disappeared. Two months later I got a card from him, postmarked Memphis, with a picture of a riverboat on it.

Hey, Pete, it read. *So far, so good. Wish me luck. Stay away from those road crews. Those bastards are a mean lot. You were lucky with me. V.*

I keep it in the top drawer of my night table. Every now and then, when the weather's thick and humid and I can't sleep, I pull the card out and jerk off, holding it in my hand. It's not as good as the real thing, not by a long shot. But it helps me remember that hot summer night, when an escaped con plowed my ass so good and fell asleep with my cum on his face.

YOSEMITE SAM

Iт's ONLY JUNE, but it's hotter than a motherfucker right now, some kind of fluke in the weather, and I'm just sitting in my chair watching the tube, feeling the sweat trickle down my armpits. It's Friday night, and I feel like I should go out and *do* something, hang out with the guys maybe, but I don't have it in me. This heat's really got me down. I think of what summers are like in Hoboken, the garbage cans stinking in the alleys, the asphalt going soft, having to sleep with the windows open so you hear the whores down below calling out to the johns, and when you yell at them to shut up, they yell back up to you, "Go fuck yourself."

Anyway, I hear this knock on my door, "Shave and a haircut, two bits," and I know it's Eddy, 'cause that's the way he always knocks. I get up and open the door, and sure enough, there he is, leaning against the doorway, grinning. "Aren't you going to let me in?" he says, and I say, "Sure," trying not to show how I'm feeling, how my cock is already stiffening five seconds after seeing him.

Eddy walks in, and to look at him you'd think we were never having a heat wave, he looks cool and relaxed. He's one of the Italian boys that live in the neighborhood. Years ago we used to knock heads, but my heart was never in it, he was always so fucking beautiful: black curly hair, deep brown eyes that could melt stone, a hot, tight muscular body. Yeah, he's a looker all right. What's more, the bastard knows it. He paces the room like a panther, slow, confident, his T-shirt and tight jeans hugging that sexy body of his. He stops and looks at me, and those beautiful, dark dago eyes of his don't miss nothin', they take me in, size me up, and know whatever he wants from me, I'll give it. He raises his arms and stretches slowly. "I was just in the neighborhood, Andy, so I thought I'd drop by and say hi."

"Have a seat."

He shakes his head. "Nah, I can't stay long. I got a date with Angela." He sighs. "A beautiful girl, Angela. A knockout." He screws his face up. "But these Catholic girls. They just don't put out. And man, have I got a load tonight."

It don't take an Einstein to figure where this is going. "That's a tough break," I say, acting like I don't give a fuck.

He smiles. "I was hoping you'd help me out."

"I dunno, Eddy. Not tonight."

But he's already unbuckling his belt, and in half a minute he's got his jeans and shorts down around his ankles. He just leans against the wall and looks at me, stroking that big, gorgeous uncut dick of his, his balls hanging low and sweaty from the heat. "Come on, Andy," he croons to me. "Suck me off. You know you want to."

And the fucker's right, of course, I want to in the worst way. We sure as hell've been through this routine often enough. In no time flat I'm down on my knees in front of him and he's fucking my face, pumping that Italian salami in and out of my mouth. I grab his balls and squeeze them, not too hard, just play with them. Eddy knows I love his balls, how low and meaty they are, and soon I'm sucking on them too, bathing my tongue around them, letting them fill my mouth while I stroke Eddy's cock. Eddy grabs me by my hair and pulls my head back, and then crams my mouth full of dickmeat again. He's pumping his hips hard now, stuffing his fuckstick all the way down my throat, his balls slapping against my chin. I take it all, rubbing my nose deep into his pubes, rolling my tongue around all that meat in my mouth. I grab his ass and squeeze; it feels smooth under my hands, and I can feel the muscle clench tight as he drives his dick down my throat. I got my cock out too and I'm jacking off hard, now, in time with Eddy.

Eddy had a load to drop, all right, 'cause in no time at all he's starting to moan, and he pumps his hips faster now. His balls are pulled up tight to his body, his dick is rock hard and ready to shoot and then it happens. He lets out this yell, pulls his crank out of my mouth, and shoots a monster load over my face. I mean gobs of the stuff are squirting out of his cum slit, I feel it on my eyes, my nose, in my mouth. He grabs hold of his dick and rubs my face with it. I put it back in my mouth and give it a few good sucks more, just to get my nut off. And it works, because I'm shooting now, I feel my cum, all hot and sticky, oozing down my hand and between my fingers.

After a couple of seconds, I get up, get a paper towel, and wipe off my face and hand. Eddy pulls up his pants and buckles his belt.

"Why don't you stay a little while, Eddy?" I say. "Have a beer with me."

Eddy smiles and then shakes his head. "I can't, pal. Angela's waiting."

"Angela ain't going anywhere. It won't fucking kill her if you're fifteen minutes late."

Eddy shrugs. "Some other time, okay?"

I give it up. "Yeah, sure." And he's out the door.

The next morning I'm at my job. I work in this garage over on 14th Street, and my boss, Vinnie, is this man who's got no class; he yells at everyone and then wonders why everybody hates his guts. And the heat's even worse than yesterday. I'm in the pit with this heap of a car above me, and I'm covered with grease and sweat and thinking about another summer in Hoboken and what that's going to be like. And I'm thinking about Eddy, too, and last night, and getting more and more pissed off about how the fucker is just using me, how he's got no respect for me. And Vinnie calls me into his office and starts screaming about the two other cars I haven't had a chance to get at, and my mind goes blank. All I see is this calendar Vinnie's got hanging on the wall, put out by some auto parts company. It's got a picture of this huge fucking cliff of rock, and this waterfall coming down next to it, with this creek below, and these trees. I ignore Vinnie and walk up to the calendar, and it says under the picture, "Half Dome, Yosemite Park," and I look at the picture again and wonder what it must be like to feel that waterfall come pouring down on my head. Vinnie yells, "Are you listening to me?" and I say, "Fuck you, asshole," and walk out the door.

George, the other mechanic, is out by the pumps. George is smart, he reads books; so I ask him, "Hey, George, where's Yosemite?" and he looks at me like what planet am I from? and says, "Where's what?" I spell it for him, and he laughs, but not like Vinnie would, like I'm some kind of dumb fuck, and he says, "That's Yo-sem-i-tee, not Yo-se-mite. And it's in California." That afternoon I clear out my savings and the next morning I'm in my car, off to California.

I don't waste any time, and in four days I'm in Yosemite Park.

And it's like the calendar picture, all right, these mother loving mountains, and pine trees, and monster waterfalls. Only a ranger tells me that if I stand under one it'll crack my skull open, so I don't.

I sleep in my car that night, like I been doing the past four days, and early the next morning I go to this building called "Park Headquarters." Even though it's early, there're some people already there, some guy in these puke green shorts with his wife and these two kids who are running around trashing the place. The guy's talking to the ranger, so I stand behind him waiting for him to get done. The woman's screaming at the kids, and they're screaming back at her, and I'm thinking maybe it would be a good idea if *they* stood under the waterfall and let it crack their skulls open, when this other dude walks in. I can't take my eyes off of him, he's fucking beautiful. He's got red hair and a beard, broad shoulders, powerful arms, arms that can wrap around you and squeeze slowly, pulverize you, only he wouldn't do that, I could tell right then just glancing at him, because he looks, I don't know, *calm*, at ease. He looks like one of the mountains here, I think. He's wearing a T-shirt that says "Go Climb A Rock," and I'd like to climb *his* rock. I can see it through those tiny shorts he's wearing; the bulge is hard to miss. And his legs bunch up with muscles, his ass behind those shorts looks hard and smooth, like Half Dome. This guy belongs here, I think. He's a wild man, I can tell. And just when I think that, he turns and looks at me, and his eyes are this blue like I've never seen before, lighter than sky, more like deep, clear water. I could fall into those eyes and drown and be happy about it. He gives me this smile and my heart starts hammering, and I wonder if he's reading my thoughts, because right now, in my mind, I'm on my knees cramming that big ol' dickmeat of his down my throat.

I hear this voice say, "Can I help you?" and I turn and see the ranger staring at me, the man ahead is gone now. So I try to come on like I know what's happening and I say, "Yeah, how do I get to the top of Half Dome? Can I get there from here?"

The ranger says, "Sure, but it's a pretty long hike." He pulls out this map and starts pointing out these trails I'm supposed to take, and I pretend like I know what the fuck he's talking about, but I'm lost, man, I'm over my head. I never seen a map like this, it's sure

no city map, and I can't make out what the fuck those little
squiggly lines are. This guy's copping an attitude, I think, he must
be getting a big kick out of this. He looks at me, and I feel like I
got "Dumb Fuck from Hoboken" tattooed on my head, and I start
feeling real low, like maybe this wasn't such a good idea coming
out here after all.

I hear this voice behind me say, "I'm backpacking up that way.
Maybe we can hike together." I turn and it's that fucking beautiful guy again, only he's right next to me now, and those blue, blue
eyes are looking at me, and they're friendly and open.

"Yeah, sure," I say, trying to hide the fact that my chest feels
so tight I can't hardly breathe.

He holds out his hand and says, "I'm Sam," and I take it and
his hand is warm and firm. "I'm Andy," I say, and there's something that's going on, I don't know, this spark between us. He
smiles, and it's not, like, *civilized*; there's an animal in that smile,
a wolf maybe, and I feel my cock stirring and I wonder if he meant
it the way I'm taking it.

So we leave, and Sam gets in his truck, and I follow behind in
my car until we get to this parking lot, and he starts strapping on
his backpack. Sam looks at me kind of funny and says, "Aren't you
going to bring anything, any water or food?"

I feel my face turning red, because, believe it or not, I hadn't
even thought about that. Think, dummy, I tell myself. It's not like
there're going to be any delis up on Half Dome. But Sam just
laughs and says, "Don't sweat it. I got us both covered."

The trail starts a little ways away, and right away it starts getting steep. It's tough going, I'm not used to all this walking, but
after a while the trail evens out again and things get easier. Sam
asks me why I wanted to hike to Half Dome and I tell him all about
Hoboken and Vinnie and the calendar picture. Sam throws back
his head and laughs and says, "I thought only I did things like
that."

Every now and then we pass by pools, some right next to the
trail, others a little off in the distance. I don't say nothing, but I
think about Sam splashing in that pool, naked, with a big hard-
on waiting for me. We start climbing again, for a long time, now,
and the sun's getting pretty hot. It sounds real good when Sam
finally suggests we break for lunch. We find a sunny rock, over-

looking another pool. Sam drops his pack and sits down. I sit next to him. He reaches in his pack, brings out a couple of sandwiches and hands one over to me. I feel kind of bad taking his food, so I say no. Sam prods me in the chest with the sandwich. "Come on, don't be a jerk," he says. "Take it." When I don't do nothing, he says, "Look, I have plenty of food. I always pack too much. So take it, all right?" I don't fight it any more and I take the sandwich. It tastes great, and I wolf it down.

I lean back on the rock and look at the water, and suddenly I start laughing.

"What?" Sam asks.

I shake my head. "Nothing."

"No, tell me."

I feel embarrassed, but I tell him. "When I was a kid, I used to watch these cartoons on the tube. There was this little red-headed fucker named Yosemite Sam who was always trying to nail Bugs Bunny's ass." I grin at him. "That's who you are. Yosemite Sam."

Sam grins back. "Dwat that Wabbit!"

I laugh. "No, you dummy, that's Elmer Fudd." Sam starts laughing with me, and it's a long time before we stop.

After a while, we start hiking again, and I feel like I'm fucking flying now, which is weird because the trail is steeper than ever. It's almost all rock, and I have to pull myself up by my hands in some places. This blows my mind; I should be getting pretty wasted, but I got this adrenalin pump. Sam seems to feel it too, 'cause he's running up the trail ahead of me, jumping from rock to rock like a mountain goat.

Finally, I turn a corner in the trail and just stop; there's ol' Half Dome, only it's not some far off picture in a calendar, it's hanging over me like some skyscraper in New York. I bend my head back and look all the way to the top; these two long cables dangle down along the side to the bottom of the cliff. Sam's at the foot, holding on to one of them. He's got his backpack off, and it's leaning against a big rock. He waves to me to come over, and when I do, he hands the cable to me.

I look at him. "What the hell am I supposed to do with that?"

"Climb to the top with it."

"You got to be shitting me."

Sam laughs. "It's easy." He grabs hold with both hands and

starts walking up the side of the cliff. After a while he looks down at me. "Come on," he shouts, "You some kind of pussy? Get a move on!"

I don't fucking like this, man. This was not in the game plan. But Sam is way above me now, and there's no way I'm going to let him think I'm chicken. I grab a cable and start climbing like I saw him do. I go a lot slower, and soon Sam is out of sight, over the top. Once I slip on some loose rocks and there ain't nothing but me holding onto that cable with my hands, swinging like Tarzan. Sweet Jesus, I pray, get me out of here; and my feet find the rock again and I go on climbing. After what seems like one mother of a long time, I crawl over the edge of the cliff and I'm on top of Half Dome.

Not far away I see a pair of shorts and a T-shirt in a pile on the ground. I hear a long, crazy howl, and there's Sam off in the distance, buck naked, arms out wide, making the goddamnedest noises. I feel the wildness too; it's just from being here, man, on top of the fucking world, with nothing but sky around you, and the sun beating down, and the wind blowing hard, and in two seconds I'm bare-assed too. I open my mouth and let out this mother of a howl, and the wind picks it up and bounces it off the rocks and it echoes back to me.

I run over to Sam thinking I'll take him from behind, wrestle him to the ground that way. But he hears me, and in the last second he spins around and grabs me, kicks my legs out, and I'm on my back with him sitting on me, my arms pinned down. His dick just lies there on my chest, and it's a beauty, long and thick, with a big mushroom head, and bright orange pubic hair above it. The hair continues up, gets darker, branches left and right when it reaches his chest. He's grinning down at me, and he looks more like a wolf than ever. He sees me eyeing that fuckmeat of his, and it slowly gets hard; soon it's sticking straight up, inches away from my face. His balls are red and meaty, and they hang low, resting on my skin. Sam begins moving his hips from side to side, and his cock rubs up and down on my chest. He reaches back behind him and grabs my cock, which is rock hard, too, and begins stroking it. "Yeah," he grins, "I knew you'd have a big one."

Sam bends down and kisses me, and his tongue goes in my mouth, deep, and he stretches out on top of me, so that his whole body is covering mine. He grinds his hips, and I feel his skin rub against mine, slippery with sweat. I reach down and grab both our cocks together, and stroke, our two dickmeats fused into one giant fuck muscle. I start eating out Sam's armpit, it's all sweaty from the hike, I smell that smell of a man's body, taste that special taste, and it's fucking driving me wild; I can't drink enough of it. I lift up his other arm and bury my mouth again into the sweaty pit. Sam's going crazy, too, and he breaks away. He starts tonguing my body, biting my nipples first, then kissing my belly, going lower and lower. He grabs my cock, looks up at me and grins, and then plunges down, taking the whole thing in at once. Fucking A, I never felt like this before, I can feel his tongue wrap around my dick, slurping it up, sucking on it, nipping my dickhead. This guy is a primo cocksucker, and I start pumping away, fucking Sam's face hard now.

Without slowing down, Sam swings his body around and over me. I look up and see that monster fuckstick of his above my face, those juicy, low-hanging balls dangling right above my mouth. The smell of dick fills my nose; I breathe deep to take it all in. I open my mouth and begin giving Sam's nuts a good bath with my tongue, licking them both sloppily, and then taking the whole sack of skin in my mouth. God, do I love balls! I suck on them greedily, rolling them around with my tongue. I move up to Sam's crank, licking it with slow, wet slides up and down the shaft. I grab hold of the thick dickmeat, and flick my tongue quickly over the head. Sam's really getting off, he's sucking me harder than ever while I'm doing this to him. I squeeze his cock, a drop of pre-cum oozes out of the cum slit, and I lap it up. I plunge up and take the whole dick down my throat. Sam goes fucking crazy. He groans and his body starts thrashing around on top of me like a fucking bronco. He starts pumping his hips like a piston, and I feel that dickmeat slide in and out of my throat, those balls of his bouncing off my face.

He breaks away, gasping. "I've got to have a piece of that ass of yours," he growls, and he grabs my legs and spreads them open. He spits on his hand and reaches down and begins rubbing a finger up and down my ass. I keep beating off while he's doing this. I feel his finger go in, to the first knuckle, then the second, and I feel I could pop my cork just from this alone. "Oh, man," I groan. "I want you to slam into me hard."

Sam pulls his finger out and gives me that grin of his. "Don't worry about it, my friend." He spits again into his hand.

I prop myself up on my elbows. "Hold off for a second, will you?" I get up, run to my jeans, and pull a rubber out of my wallet. I run back to Sam and give it to him.

He laughs. "Here's a guy who doesn't bring any food or water with him, but he has a rubber."

"I always carry one with me," I say, embarrassed. "Just in case."

"Sure, buddy," Sam says, grinning. He hands it back to me. "You do the honors."

I grab Sam's thick cock and slowly roll the rubber down the shaft. He spits on his hand again, and works it up and down his dick. He leans back on his arms, and I ease myself down until I feel the dickhead work itself inside my ass. I slowly lower myself until his dickmeat fills me completely.

"Yeah," he groans. "That's right." I wrap my legs around him, and he pulls my face to his, frenching me while he pumps away at my ass. His strokes are long and easy at first, and I hold on, getting off on the ride. He gives me a push, and I'm on my back now, and he's ramming home faster and faster. I reach down and feel his balls bouncing against my ass, feel the shaft go in and out. His face is sweating now, those blue eyes gleaming fiercely, his mouth open and breathing hard. I'm stroking my own cock, and when he bends down for a second and bites my nipple hard, I almost fucking lose it right there. Sam's beginning to groan now, I can feel his body getting tighter, the moans are getting longer, and I know it won't be long before he busts his nut. He pulls out almost all the way, and then plunges his cock deep inside, and that pops his cork for him, all right; he cries out and his body starts shuddering all over. It don't take long before I drop my load too, I feel the cum spurt out, and right away Sam bends down and takes the rest of it in his mouth. He sucks me greedily, draining my load out of my balls, and I'm yelling like a son of a bitch myself.

We lie next to each other on the rock, and I can't move, man, I feel like every bit of energy has been sucked out of me by Sam. The sun is beating down on me, and all I see is blue sky above. I just want to stay like this forever.

Sam sits up and begins rubbing my chest. "You want to stay

with me tonight?"

"You got room for me?"

"I'll fucking make room."

"Sure."

We get up, and in a couple of minutes we're climbing down Half Dome. I don't know how long I'll stay out here in California, or if I'll ever go back to Hoboken. Fuck it. Right now, I'm just thinking about the next day or so hanging out with Yosemite Sam. I look down as Sam swings down the face of the cliff, yelling like a son of a bitch. I start yelling too, and our voices bounce off the rocks around us like there were a hundred guys around us instead of just us two.

SWEET YOUNG ASS

THERE'S A slight breeze blowing in through the cab window, cooling off some of the sweat I've been working up. It ain't the only thing blowing. I reach up and stretch, locking my fingers together, and pull my knees wider apart. They can only go so far with my jeans down around my ankles. I look down at the back of Eddy's head, watching it twist back and forth as I fuck his mouth with long, slow strokes. "Hell, Eddy," I laugh. "I do believe you're getting bald."

Eddy stops his sucking and looks up, still holding my cock in his hand. He gives me one of his easy, good ol' boy smiles. "You should be careful what you say to me while your dick's in my mouth," he growls.

I grin. "Sorry. Didn't mean to break your stride." I scratch my beard and settle back into the truck's seat. "Go ahead. Don't let me stop you."

Eddy's blue eyes gleam. I swear, somewhere back in Eddy's family tree some great-granddaddy must have fucked a wolf, 'cause I can see the family resemblance now. He slowly runs his tongue up the length of my dickmeat, sucking gently on the head, tonguing my cum slit. It always excites the hell out of me watching my dickmeat pump the face of a man as handsome as Eddy. Without any warning, he plunges down, swallowing all eight and a half inches. I feel the softness of Eddy's beard press down against my low-hangers. Up and down his mouth goes, his tongue wrapping around my dick, squeezing it, caressing it. Sweet Jesus, can that boy suck cock! It's one of his most endearing qualities. I look up at the cab's roof, letting the sensations sweep over me, and start giving out some mighty groans to show Eddy my appreciation.

Eddy's sucking on my balls now, first the left one, then the right, rolling each one around in his mouth, while he strokes my fuckstick slowly. He's humping his fist with the same, even tempo, and I reach down to give him a helping hand. His dickmeat is slick with spit and precum and slides in and out of my hand as easy as butter on a hot skillet.

My other hand rubs and strokes across Eddy's chest, feeling those pumped-up hard pecs and the soft fur that covers them. I grab his left nipple between thumb and forefinger and squeeze hard. Eddy, his mouth full of my balls, grunts his approval, and I slap the back of his head. "Didn't your mama never teach you not to talk with your mouth full?" I grin. Eddy laughs and I pull his face up to mine, shoving my tongue deep into his mouth. Eddy rolls over on top of me, and his muscular arms wrap around me in a powerful bear hug. I feel his hard flesh pressed tight against mine, the sweaty skin sliding back and forth across my chest, his thick dick dry humping my belly. I breathe in the strong man-smell of Eddy's sweat; we've both just gotten off an eight hour shift of logging redwoods and we reek. I work a finger into Eddy's tight bunghole with excruciating slowness, up to the third knuckle. My finger is encased in warm velvet. I wiggle it, pushing against the prostate, and Eddy goes fucking crazy, thrashing around in the cab, squirming against me, groaning loud enough to wake the dead. This boy needs a serious fucking.

Still kissing Eddy, I pull my finger out of his ass and grope in the glove compartment for a condom. I roll one down my shaft, Eddy shifts his hips up, and we resume playing dueling tongues as I slowly impale him. I fuck Eddy with short, quick thrusts, and he pumps his hips to meet me, matching me stroke for stroke. My hand's wrapped around Eddy's thick shaft, jerking him off like there's hell to pay.

Fucking in the front seat of a truck cab ain't the most comfortable way to get off. Eddy's head is bent down to keep from bumping the roof, and the stick shift keeps hitting me in the leg. But neither of us is complaining. I settle into a steady rhythm of plowing ass, Eddy's face just inches away from mine. I look deep into those wild blue eyes, and he stares back at me, his eyes narrowed in concentration, his lips pulled back into a soundless snarl. A low, half-whimper comes out of his mouth, and then another. I spit in my hand and continue stroking his dickmeat. The whimper turns into a long, trailing groan. I stroke faster now, and he groans again, loud. I squeeze his nipple and that does the trick. Eddy arches his back, and his body begins shuddering as he shoots his load. The first squirt gets me right in the face, just below my left eye. The next two hit me on the chin. Eddy's bellowing like a damn bullmoose, and the squirts just keep on a-cumming. I'm soaked with the stuff before he's done.

I shove my dick once more hard up its entire length into Eddy's ass and that does the trick for me. I groan loudly, and Eddy plants his mouth roughly on top of mine. He tongues me damn well down to my throat as my jizz shoots into the condom up his ass. There's a lot of thrashing about, a lot of crashing into ashtrays and door handles, until finally, things quiet down. Eddy softly licks his cum off my face as I lie back, eyes closed, feeling the late afternoon breeze blow in through the window. I can hear the leaves outside rustling, and, farther off in the distance, the buzz of the chain saws of the afternoon shift.

After a few minutes, Eddy pushes himself up. "I gotta take a leak," he says and climbs out of the cab. I watch him lazily, admiring his fine, tight ass, as he stands on the road edge buck naked and pisses down the hillside.

His body suddenly stiffens. "Hey, Dale," he calls over his shoulder towards me. "Come over here."

I'm almost drifting off to sleep now. "Why?" I ask irritably.

"Just get over here, goddamn it!"

Grumbling, I push out of the truck's cab and walk over to where Eddy's standing. "What's up?" I growl.

Eddy points down below and I follow the direction of his finger. Way down below I can see the work crew cutting away at the redwoods growing on the valley floor. But that's not what's got Eddy's attention. He's pointing closer up, where the logging road winds along the side of the hill before it climbs to the spot where we're standing. And now I see what's got his attention. Halfway down the ridge, by the side of the road, there's a man lying on his belly, snapping pictures of the tree-cutting operation going on below him. A backpack lies by his side.

I look at Eddy. "What do you think he's up to?" I ask.

Eddy shrugs. We watch the dude for a moment longer, not saying anything. "I bet he's a tree-hugger," Eddy finally says. I nod, keeping my eyes on him. "I think you're right." At this distance it's hard to tell, but he looks like he's not much more than a kid. I turn to Eddy, grinning. "Let's take him!"

The last few hundred feet, I switch off the engine and coast around the curve. The tree-hugger's still there, stretched out on a small patch of grass a little ways off from the road, still snapping pictures. I look at Eddy and put a finger to my lips. We climb out of the truck and creep over towards him.

We get to just a few feet away from him. "What the hell do you think you're doing!" I bark.

This gets the desired effect. The guy jumps up and whirls around, facing us with wide eyes. I can see he's young, all right, early twenties maybe, clean-shaven, but with a shaggy mane of dark blonde hair. His cut-offs show two powerfully muscled legs. Most likely a mountain biker, I think. I still got the picture in my head of how tight his ass looked when he was on his belly. The kid stares at us, saying nothing.

"The man asked what you're doing," Eddy says quietly, his wolf's eyes squinting. Eddy can look real mean when he wants to.

The kid swallows. "I was watching the loggers down below."

"Yeah," I say. "And taking pictures, too."

The kid's eyes dart to my face, then Eddy's, then back to mine again. It's clear he wishes badly he was somewhere else. I can't help but notice how good-looking he is, with a firm jaw, alert brown eyes, tight body. "Look," he says, his voice low. "I'm just taking a hike. Photography's a hobby of mine."

I narrow my eyes, doing my best Clint Eastwood. "What's your name?"

The kid meets my gaze, and, I have to give him credit, holds it steadily. "Mark," he says.

"This is private property, Mark," I rap. "Owned by Carolina-Pacific Lumber. You got no business being here."

"Yeah, and you guys got no business cutting down those old growth redwoods!" Mark blurts. "There's a court injunction forbidding you from doing it!"

Well, that sure as hell clears up any doubts about whether or not he's a tree-hugger. I turn to Eddy. "I think we ought to take him down to the foreman's trailer." Which is pure bluff. I have no intention of turning this kid over to anyone, much less those fucking animals down below. I just want to throw a scare in him.

The low rumble of a truck comes from around the bend behind us, and me and Eddy turn to look in its direction. The kid, quick to grab the opportunity, sprints off the road and jumps down the side of the ridge, half falling, half running, until he's swallowed up by the trees. A logging truck comes around the curve, loaded down with redwoods, all old growth. Mike, the driver, toots his horn and waves, and Eddy and me wave back. We watch the truck round the next bend in a cloud of dust.

Eddy nods towards the kid's backpack. "Our buddy seems to have left something behind."

I grin. "You want to go look for him?"

Eddy gives me a disgusted look. "Are you crazy? I ain't climbing down that hill. I'm going home to a cold beer."

I'm already sliding down the hill. "You ain't going nowhere with the keys to the truck in my pocket," I call over my shoulder. "You can either wait or come with me."

Behind me, I hear Eddy curse. He starts scrambling down the hill after me.

We find Mark just a little ways off, sitting on a log with his right boot and sock off. His ankle is already beginning to swell badly.

"Looks like you had a little accident," I say mildly.

Mark glares at me but says nothing.

"Come on," I say. "Me and Eddy'll get you back to the truck."

When we get to the road, Mark shakes us off like so many flies. He hobbles to his backpack and pulls out an ace bandage.

"Get in the truck," I say. "You can do that back at our place."

Mark begins wrapping the bandage around his ankle. "Just leave me alone. I can get back on my own."

"Yeah, right. It's eight miles back to the main road."

"That's my problem." Mark stands up. He takes a step and grimaces with pain.

"Don't be a jerk," I say impatiently. "Get in the damn truck."

Mark starts limping down the road. He flips me off without looking back.

I shrug. "Suit yourself." I open the truck door and climb in. I look at Eddy. "You comin' or are you walkin' too?"

Eddy glances at Mark and then climbs into the truck. I start the engine and begin pulling away.

"Wait!" Mark shouts. I stop. The kid is blushing now, and his eyes are shooting daggers at me. Damn if he don't look sexier than a motherfucker. I feel my cock stir. "You're right," he says.

"There's no way I can make it back on my own." I can tell it's killing him to admit it.

I throw open the door. "Hop in."

Mark's face twitches, and, in spite of himself, he grins. "Hop is about the only thing I can do right now," he says.

Mark takes a pull from his beer. He's sitting in a chair by the fire, with his foot propped up on a stool. "What those fuckers you work for are doing is illegal, you know. Like I said, there's a court injunction against logging old growth in this area."

I give him a long, deadpan look. "What if me and Eddy told you we agree with you?"

"Yeah, right."

"We do, you know." I nod towards his camera. "Look, we could just pull the film out of your camera right now, if we wanted to. You think you could stop us?"

Mark glares at me. He's a suspicious li'l fucker, all right. "Then why were you guys out there cutting down the trees along with all your asshole friends?"

The kid is getting my goat. "Because, you little college punk," I say slowly, "if we refuse, we get our asses fired. And logging's the only thing we know how to do." I glare back at him until he finally looks away. "Eddy and me grew up in this area. Our daddies were loggers. So were our granddaddies. But this shit is new, they're clearcutting everything. They're killing the land. In twenty years there ain't going to be nothing left to log."

"Hell, man," Eddy chimes in. "If those pictures will slow the cutting down, we *want* you to get through with them."

Mark gives a short laugh. "Great. You just get me to my car tomorrow and I'll do the rest." He kills the rest of his bottle and scans the room. "You guys live here together?" he asks. I nod. I can almost hear what he's thinking, that there's only one bedroom in the place. He looks at me again, his eyes bold. "You guys lovers?"

Eddy shifts in his seat. "You ask a lot of questions," he growls.

I return his stare. "Yeah, we're lovers," I say levelly. "You got a problem with that?"

Mark shakes his head. "Not at all." He grins, and after a beat of five, adds. "As a matter of fact, I swing that way myself."

There's a long silence while me and Eddy chew on this little piece of information. I give Mark a hard steady look, trying to keep a poker face, but I can feel my heart pounding. Mark looks back at me, the firelight flickering across his young, handsome face, his eyes gleaming, his lips pulled back into an easy smile. Damn! These kids nowadays are all so sure we'll go to hell and back for a piece of their ass. The trouble is, they're right. At least when they look like Mark. My dick starts stiffening under my jeans, and I shift in my chair so as not to give Mark the satisfaction of noticing. "So what do you want me to do about that?" I grunt.

Mark's grin widens. "Oh, I don't know. Maybe we can all think of something." He pulls his T-shirt off and then slowly unzips his cutoffs and pulls them down, carefully lifting his right ankle to kick them off. He sits back in the chair again, looking at both of us with a calm expression. Even half-erect, his cock is impressive: thick, meaty, with a large, mushroom head. Firelight dances over his veined, slightly twitching dickmeat and the fleshy balls beneath it. I glance at Eddy, but his eyes are fixed with a hungry gleam on Mark's naked body. Eddy always was a pig for dick. But hell, so am I. Eddy begins rubbing his own dick under the heavy fabric of his jeans. He shoots a quizzical glance in my direction, and I nod agreement. Yeah, Eddy, let's go for it.

Mark sees my nod and laughs. "Hell, with my ankle like it is, I can't come to you. If this is going to happen, you guys are going to have to come over here."

I don't do nothing for a couple of beats. Don't want the kid to think I'm too eager. Finally I stand up, walk over to Mark and stand in front of him, my crotch inches from his face. "Okay, fucker," I growl. "Now what?"

Mark reaches over and slips his hand under my shirt, sliding it across my belly. His fingers hook around the top of my jeans and he draws me closer. He places his mouth over the rough fabric just above my cock and gently bites. With his other hand, Mark begins pumping his dickmeat. I reach down and squeeze his left nipple, not gently. Mark groans. He undoes my belt buckle and unzips my fly. I just stand there, letting him do all the work. He's no longer wearing that sly smile; he has an expression I know well: dick hunger, and it gets my dick granite hard knowing it's me who's put that aching look on his face. He pulls my jeans down to my knees, and then my shorts. My cock springs to full attention. I glance over towards Eddy and see he's already whipped out his own dick and is furiously beating off.

Mark reaches over and squeezes my cock gently; a little pre-cum pearl oozes through my cum slit. Mark laps it up. "My favorite flavor," he grins, looking up at me.

"Yeah," I laugh. "Rum raisin."

Mark laughs too. He runs his tongue up the length of my dick-meat, swirls it twice around the head and then swallows it all, his nose buried deep into my pubes. My knees buckle for a second, and then, holding the kid's head with both hands, I begin fucking his mouth with long, slow strokes. Mark cups my balls with his hand and squeezes them gently.

I glance over at Eddy, still on the other side of the room, still yanking his crank, those beautiful, low-hanging balls of his just bouncing to the tempo of his beat. "Hey, Eddy!" I yell. "Get your skinny ass over here!" I look down at Mark, who's looking back up at me, my cock shoved full to the base down his throat. "Eddy's always a little shy at parties," I explain.

Eddy lurches over, his jeans down around his ankles, his thick meat swinging heavily from side to side. I pull him over to me and kiss him hard, my tongue probing deep into his mouth. I spit in my hand and then wrap it around Eddy's dick, sliding it up and down the thick shaft. Eddy's blue wolf eyes narrow, and a small groan escapes from his mouth.

Mark begins tonguing Eddy's fleshy nut sac, sucking on one ball, then the other, then the two of them together. He pushes my hand aside and deep throats Eddy's dick, his mouth working its way up and down the thick shaft of meat. All the time he's fucking his own fist hard and fast. It's clear that Mark's a brother dick pig as well. After a few sucks, he returns to my meat, then back to Eddy's. I look at Eddy's and my dicks thrusting out side by side. Eddy's is red, and thicker than mine, uncut and heavily veined. A good, meaty working man's dick. Mine is longer and darker, cut, with a narrower head. Mark is giving us both masterful head, sliding his mouth up and down our cranks, while twisting his head from side to side in long, skillful strokes. The kid's amazing! Is this something they teach in college? Makes me regret dropping out of high school.

I pull Mark to his feet, and kiss him, my hands exploring his torso, pinching his nipples, playing with his ass. I lift his right arm and tongue his pit, savoring the sweet/bitter taste of man sweat. It's a taste I could get drunk on. My tongue crosses over to his left nipple and swirls around it. I nip it gently and feel Mark's body tremble under my hands. I do the same with his right nipple. My tongue slides down the smooth, hard ridges of his belly, past his stiff dick, and washes over those meaty balls of his. I take them both in my mouth and suck hard. Mark heaves a sigh just a hair's breadth shy of a groan. Holding the kid's dickmeat in my hand, my tongue runs the length of his shaft. When I get to its red, engorged head, I plunge down and swallow it all, my beard pressed tight against his balls. Mark cries out, and I dive into a frenzy of cocksucking. The kid is good at giving head, but nobody eats dick as good as I do, and I aim to prove it. I have the honor of the blue collar working class to uphold.

Eddy reaches into a table drawer, pulls out a condom, and slips it on. He wraps his powerful arms around Mark from behind, and slowly impales his ass. Mark grimaces and Eddy pauses a bit before he continues working his dick in. It don't take long before he's plowing Mark's sweet young ass hard, driving his dickmeat home with ball-slammin' force.

My mouth glides up and down the shaft of the kid's dickmeat, my head twisting from side to side to increase the sensation for him. Between the two of us, the kid is getting worked over good. I can see he's well on his way to losing it big time. Mark's groans are bouncing off the rafters now, and his body is trembling like a leaf in a gale force wind. He twists his head around and shoots Eddy a wild-eyed look, sweat streaming down his face. Eddy plants his mouth over Mark's and tongues him for all he's worth, at the same time reaching down and twisting the kid's nipples hard. Mark bucks between us like a bronco in heat, but we hold on, Eddy slamming hard into his ass, me feeding on his dick. I come up for air, sliding my spit-and-pre-cum slicked hand up and down Mark's crank. I feel his balls in my hand tighten up, and I know he's about ready to shoot.

A couple of more strokes and he's over the edge. Mark yells loud enough to bring the roof down, and a mighty load of jism squirts out of his dickhead, splattering against my face and chest. Eddy roars soon after as he squirts his load into the condom up Mark's ass, his arms wrapped tight enough around the kid to damn near squeeze the air out of him. It just takes a few more strokes of my fist around my dick before I'm blasting my load halfway across the room as well. The two of them sink down beside me, and we kiss, Mark and Eddy licking the jism off my face. We collapse together in a heap on the rug by the fire, and stay like that until the sky through the window starts turning light.

We drop the kid off at his car the next morning. "Take good care of those pictures," I tell him. "Not all of us agree with what's happening."

Mark and Eddy hug, and then Mark climbs into his car. I stick my head in the window and kiss him hard, my tongue slipping into his mouth. "Come back here some time soon," I growl, "or I'll have to head south and hunt you down."

Mark grins. "Wild horses couldn't keep me away," he says. He pulls away, Eddy and me just standing there, watching, as his car disappears into the distance.

"Some fun, eh?" Eddy says, winking at me.

I look at him and grin. "Hell, yeah, Eddy!" We laugh and climb back into the truck.

HORNY BUS PUNK

I SEE HIM the moment I walk in on the bus. Of course the bus is a damn cattle car, every square inch packed with sweating, tired, pissed-off people who have just gotten off work and want only to go home and veg out in front of the tube. I'm certainly not any different. But between the jostling heads and shuffling bodies, for a second there's a space where I spot him, slouched in his seat, looking straight ahead with half-lidded, bored eyes. He's wearing a torn, grease-stained T-shirt, with a pack of cigarettes rolled up in the sleeve. His biceps are impressive, he must work out; tattooed crudely across the left one is the name "Angela," no heart or anything, just the scrawled name. A real punk, just eighteen or nineteen years old, twenty, tops. I have a hard-on before the bus has a chance to pull away from the stop.

That's nothing unusual. All I ever am is horny, nowadays. Rico walked out on me six weeks ago, I can't say I didn't see it coming, in fact it was something of a relief. But I haven't been laid since then (and the last few times with Rico weren't exactly stellar). Though there were times when Rico knew all the right moves, and I could just spend eternity plowing that sweet brown ass of his, all night just doin' the horizontal bop with sweet Rico as he moved his body in such perfect rhythm to mine.

So I'm looking at this kid on the bus, with those brown liquid eyes that are right now saying "fuck you" to the world at large. His strong wide mouth is pulled back into a sneer that he's probably not even conscious of, it's just his natural expression. I notice the wet stains under his armpits and imagine burrowing my face into his smelly pits, lapping up the musty, acrid nectar of his sweat. Just looking at him, I feel the ache inside, the urge to merge so acute it's like a physical pain, and I'm *pissed*. Goddammit! What right does that handsome little bastard have to just sit there looking so hot, making me ache this way! I think of those nights with Rico again and I just want to throw back my head and howl my frustration.

I get a grip. But in spite of my better judgment I worm my way through the crowd until I'm standing next to the dude, the bulge in my crotch just inches from his face. I stare down at him, willing him to meet my glance. He does, once, when he stretches and idly looks around the bus. Our eyes lock for half a second, and I can see he's looking right through the back of my head, I don't even fuckin' exist in his eyes. He turns away and stares out the window, bored. My eyes burn holes in him, but he doesn't look back at me. Now I'm taking this very personally. Everything in the universe has shrunk down to this one hard need: that this hot, arrogant son-of-a-bitch acknowledge I exist.

We're cruising down the Sacramento Street hill at a reckless pace; the driver is some kind of crazy cowboy, going so fast, especially with the bus packed the way it is now. All of a sudden he hits a pothole and we all go flying. I make no effort to grab the rail; I go crashing down on the kid, hard, hands out to catch myself against his tight, compact body. He notices me then, all right. "What the fuck!" he snarls. I push myself off him, kneading the muscles of his torso with absolutely no attempt at subtlety, before I straighten up to a standing position again.

His eyes burn into mine; there's murder in them. I give him my blandest smile. "Sorry," I say, in as smarmy a tone as I can muster up. I know I'm being a jerk; this kid has done nothing to me and yet I'm taking tremendous delight in bugging the holy hell out of him. I've just been frustrated too damn long, that's my problem.

My stop is at the bottom of the hill. The bus pulls over and I push my way out. Suddenly the kid bounds out of his seat and follows me out onto the sidewalk. "Hey, asshole!" he calls out to me.

I turn and face him, "Are you talking to me?" I ask him politely.

"Yeah, dickhead." He struts towards me aggressively. "I didn't like the way you grabbed me back there."

I look at him, at the black crisp curls of his hair, the dark eyes, the tight muscular body, the wide, sensual mouth. The ache sweeps over me again, and with it the rage. "You can kiss my ass," I say, turning away from him. Out of the corner of my eye I catch a quick movement. I grew up on some mean streets in Jersey City; there's very little I don't know about street fighting. I turn and block his punch easily. This catches him completely by surprise, and I can see he's left himself wide open. I don't pursue the advantage, though if I wanted to I could have coldcocked him right then and there. "Just go home," I say, disgusted, more with myself than him. Suddenly I feel very depressed.

But damn if he doesn't lunge at me again. I sidestep him, and, using his momentum against him, pivot his body around, wrapping my arm around his neck as I bring his own arm up behind him in a half-nelson. I press my body tight against his so that he can't struggle free. "I don't want to hurt you," I growl in his ear. "Will you knock it off?"

"Cocksucker!" he spits out at me, struggling futilely to get free.

All I can think about is how good his body feels pressed against me. Rico felt like this; he liked to wrestle too before we got into the wild sex that always followed. I've got a hard-on fit to split my pants open. "I'm going to let you go," I pant. "If you try anything else, I swear, I'll flatten you." I release him.

He spins around, but keeps his distance warily. At least he's got *some* native wit about him. He's panting heavily now, and his face is flushed. His eyes burn through me like lasers. This little scene could go any number of ways, depending on what I do next.

Frustration makes me reckless. I straighten up. "How would you like to earn an easy hundred bucks?" I ask.

This catches him completely off guard. "What the fuck are you talking about?" he snarls.

"Just that. How would you like a hundred bucks. Cash."

His eyes narrow into slits. "What would I have to do?" Some of the bravado is gone from his stance. I can tell he's interested.

"Let me suck your cock."

Predictably, his face hardens into contempt. "You faggot," he sneers.

I give a hard little laugh. "This faggot just whipped your ass, buddy." I straighten my tie. "Money is money. Just think about my offer before you start calling me any more names."

"Shit!" he exclaims, shaking his head. "No way!"

I shrug. "Have it your way." I turn and start walking away.

I go about a dozen steps. "A hundred and fifty bucks!" he calls out after me.

I can't help but smile. He's hooked now. I turn and face him. "I'm not going to dicker. A hundred bucks. Take it or leave it."

We look hard into each other's eyes. "I don't do nothin', right?"

he mutters.

"No," I say, smiling. "Just stand there and take it like a man. Have we got a deal?"

Another pregnant silence. He finally shrugs. "Okay," he says.

A little jolt of excitement shoots through me. "I just live up the street," I say, trying to keep my voice calm. "Just follow me."

After a few steps I turn to him. "What's your name?"

He keeps his eyes aimed straight ahead. "What difference does it make?" he mutters.

"No difference at all, I guess," I finally reply. We don't say anything else while on the street.

As soon as we're in my apartment he begins unbuckling his belt. I put my hand on his and stop him. "We don't have to rush this," I say. "Do you want a beer?"

He pulls his hand away from mine and looks at me with flat hostile eyes. "No," he says. There's an ugly little pause. "Look," he says impatiently. "Can we get this over with?"

I briefly consider calling this off. "You may not be thirsty, but I am," I say. "I'm going to get a beer." I walk into the kitchen, leaving him standing alone in the middle of the living room. I come back with a Dos Equis in my hand and sit down on the couch. I stare at him as I take a long pull from the bottle. "How did you get all that grease on your shirt? You work in a garage?"

He shifts his weight impatiently to his other leg and grimaces. "What is this shit?" he growls.

"Look," I say mildly, giving my voice just the slightest edge. "If you want the money, you're going to have to play the game my way. Otherwise you can just get your ass out right now."

He glares at me. I can almost hear the wheels turning in his brain as he gauges just how much he really wants the money. Finally he clears his throat. "No," he says. "I don't work in a garage. I got a bike, an old Kawasaki. I been trying to fix it up."

I relax back into the couch. "That's better," I say. "Now, what's your name?"

"Andy." He hitches his thumbs in his pockets.

"Hello, Andy," I say. "I'm Joe." Andy looks at me with blank eyes and says nothing. "Now what I want you to do is take your clothes off. Slowly."

Andy's eyes dart uncertainly. "I thought all I had to do was drop my pants," he protests.

"You thought wrong."

Andy stands there considering this new wrinkle. I pull my wallet out of my back pocket, take out five twenties and lay them on the end table by the couch. I don't say anything. This is all that's needed to tip the scales in my favor. Andy begins pulling off his shirt.

"No," I say. "Leave the shirt on for the time being." The thought of Andy standing buck naked in front of me except for that greasy torn T-shirt is an image almost too erotic to bear.

Andy glances at the money on the end table. He kicks off his beat-up sneakers and unbuckles his belt. He unzips his fly. His pants drop down around his ankles, and he steps out of them, kicking them aside. My heart feels like it's hammering loud enough to wake the dead. He pulls off his socks, hooks his thumbs inside the elastic band of his jockey shorts, and pulls them down and off. The shorts are frayed and lined with a couple of skid marks.

"Just stand there for a moment," I say quietly. I can hardly breathe. Andy puts his hands on his hips and sneers at me. He knows his power now; I'm sure the hunger I'm feeling registers clearly on my face. I'm beyond caring. My eyes drink him in: his sullen, beautiful face, his muscular torso bound in the torn T-shirt, the biceps bulging against the sleeves, his legs spread apart and defiant. His cock hangs between his thighs in meaty promise: substantial, uncut, thick, giving every assurance of being truly impressive when hard. His balls are low-hanging and swollen, resting like two eggs in the fleshy sac.

Sweet Jesus, I think. *It's visions like this that make me believe there is a God.* I moisten my lips. "Come over here," I say. By some miracle I keep my voice from cracking. Andy takes a few steps and stands directly in front of me, his cock and balls hanging a couple of inches from my face. I breathe deeply, taking in the sweaty man-smell of his crotch. I wrap my hand around his dick. Andy flinches slightly but offers no resistance. I pull the foreskin over the head and feel the warmth of Andy's cock spread out into my palm. I bend over and kiss the cockhead softly, the shaft next, then the balls. The musky smell is riper down there: I bury my nose in Andy's scrotum, deep in the loose folds of flesh, and fill my lungs with the pungent odor. I'm drunk already. I kiss his balls again, tenderly and then take them in my mouth, washing them with my tongue. I gently suck on them as my hand slowly strokes his dick-shaft. With the fleshy pouch still in my mouth, I glance up at Andy's face. Surprisingly, I don't see the contempt I expect. If any-thing, his expression is merely puzzled, and his eyes regard me with open curiosity. I guess he wonders what the hell I get out of all this.

Stroked by my spit-slicked hand, his dick is beginning to get hard. I roll my tongue around the cockhead, pushing it into the piss slit, and then suddenly swallow the dick whole, till my nose is buried deep in Andy's crisp, black pubes. Andy gasps and his dick immediately swells to full hardness. I begin sucking cock in earnest now, sliding my mouth up the shaft, working it with my lips, twisting my head from side to side for maximum exposure. This used to drive Rico crazy, and it seems to have the same ef-fect on Andy. He groans and seizes my head with both hands, as he drives his dick deep down my throat. His meat is both thick and long and fills my mouth completely, but I take it like a champ. If Andy feels he can intimidate me by the size of his meat, he's wrong. I feed on it voraciously, my hands sliding over his body, cupping his muscular ass, slipping under his T-shirt and knead-ing the hard flesh of his torso.

I come up for air, panting. Reaching up, I grasp Andy's T-shirt with both hands and yank savagely. There's a loud ripping noise as the cotton tears apart, revealing a torso lean and hairless, every muscle defined. The abs alone are chiseled like cut glass and feel like bands of vulcanized rubber under my hands. I yank open my belt and pull my pants down. I go back to sucking Andy's thick dickmeat as I pummel my own cock with my right hand. Andy pumps his hips rapidly, fucking my face with fierce, quick strokes. My left hand kneads his ass, feeling the muscles clench and un-clench as he drives his thick meat home. I match his rhythm pre-cisely, descending on his cockshaft just at the moment he plunges it into my throat, then withdraw as he does. Suddenly, he thrusts his dick hard down my throat and leaves it there, grinding his pelvis against my face, choking me. I look up at him and he grins back, his eyes gleaming malevolently. I grip both his nipples be-tween my thumbs and forefingers and squeeze hard. Andy yelps and pulls back. I release my grip, and we resume the old rhythm of thrust and suck as if nothing had happened.

If there's one thing I know how to do, it's suck cock. As my lips slide up and down Andy's shaft, I can sense how hard it's gotten, how Andy's balls are pulled up tight and getting ready to release their load. Andy starts making little sex noises: grunts and whimpers that are getting progressively louder and longer. Taking my cue, he pinches his nipples as he thrusts his hips more urgently, the strokes getting faster and deeper. His dick throbs in my mouth like something with a life of its own. I can tell that in a couple of seconds he's going to squirt. He gives a long trailing groan.

I quickly pull away, releasing his cock. "What did you do that for?" he complains. He reaches down to grab his dick and finish the job. I knock his hand away.

"This is my show, Andy," I say. "Don't interfere. I'll get you off when I'm good and ready." Andy gives me a hard, angry look. The kid wants to squirt his load *bad;* for a second I think he's going to try to grab his dick again. But he keeps his hands at his side, clenching and unclenching his fists.

His dick juts out in front of my face, red and slippery; I drink it in with my eyes. I can see why a man's meat is sometimes called a "root." That's what Andy's looks like: gnarled, thick, knotted with veins. Something organic and earthy, the source of a man's strength. I just want to stay on my knees and worship it with my mouth all day.

I wrap my hand around Andy's cock and squeeze gently; a pearl of pre-cum oozes out and I lap it up. Andy sighs. I run my tongue along Andy's dick teasingly, flicking it lightly. I take his dick into my mouth again and with excruciating slowness begin nibbling my lips down the length of the shaft. Andy trembles and his knees buckle slightly. I tug gently on his balls, rolling them tenderly in my hand. I always love the balls of young men, fertile jizz factories always looking for an opportunity to squirt. Andy's lay heavily in my hand, and I can feel their ripeness, how much they're *bursting* with spunk. It would take only the slightest provocation to trigger the whole mechanism, release Andy's creamy load down the warm, wet confines of my throat. Carefully, gently, I resume sucking Andy off, drawing him once more to the edge.

Andy's body begins to shudder. I stop immediately. "No, please," Andy pleads. "Don't stop, I gotta shoot." His face is twisted in an agony of frustration. He reaches again for his dick.

I seize his wrist. "I told you this is *my* game!" I say sharply. Andy glowers at me, but behind the anger I can see the ache. He really does want to shoot bad; it must be torture for the kid to wait like this. With an effort, I suppress a smile. "Lie down on the couch," I tell him. Andy hesitates. "You want to get off or not?" I ask, putting an edge to my voice.

Andy reluctantly lowers himself onto the couch. He stretches his legs out into a V and leans back, watching me expectantly. His expression is still hostile, but the contempt is no longer there. Neither is the cockiness. For the moment, he's as much along for the ride as I am. His dick is red, hard, and shiny with saliva and pre-cum, and his balls are pulled up tight. I take my beer and tilt the bottle over him. A foamy stream flows down his hard belly and spills over his cock, like mountain rapids. I look at his face; his eyes are half shut, and his lips are parted. A lock of dark hair falls across his forehead. His beauty is like a knife in my gut. I lean down and run my tongue across his torso, through the foam, and down the length of his dick shaft. I lie between his legs and take his balls in my mouth again, washing them with my tongue. Reaching up, I pour another stream of beer down his torso. It trickles into my mouth, and I lap it up thirstily.

My tongue wanders down the hairy path to Andy's asshole, and stays there for a visit. I lick it greedily. Andy shifts his body, pushing up with his knees so that I can get better access. He gives a long sigh that's just a hair's breadth away from being a groan. I return to Andy's balls, wash my tongue over them, and then slowly slide my tongue up the length of his dick shaft. Andy groans again. My tongue traces a wet path up Andy's torso and flicks his left nipple, while I pinch his right one between my thumb and forefinger. Andy's body squirms under me. I lift his left arm and burrow my face into his pit, just like I fantasized back on the bus. His sweat is pungent and ripe on my tongue, intoxicating to my nose. I nuzzle deep into his other armpit, as I slowly stroke his slippery dick-meat with my hand. Andy's groans grow louder. I lift my head and look at him. Andy looks back with desperate eyes. In the space of a few minutes, all the power has shifted over to me; now it's Andy with the ache that he hopes I'll satisfy.

I decide to give him his release. I speed up the tempo of my strokes. Andy trembles and his balls pull up tight against his body.

I can feel the first throb of his cock. I put my finger down between his nuts and press hard.

This does the trick. Andy arches his back and cries out. The first gush of jizz squirts out of his dick and splatters against his chin. His dick spews another load, and then another. Andy thrashes on the couch like a wild man, still bellowing at top volume. His dick throbs in my hand as spurt after spurt of spunk gushes out. By the time he's through shooting, Andy's torso is caked.

I stroke my dick fast with my cum-smeared hand. Andy is sprawled out on my couch, gasping, his eyes closed. A drop of his jizz hangs from his chin, another from his cockhead. I drink in the sight of Andy's naked, cum-soaked body and feel the excitement rise up inside. It takes just a few strokes to bring me to the brink of popping my own cork, and I stand up to let 'er rip. With a cry, I shoot; my spunk arcs across the air and lands on Andy's chest, mingling with his own spermy deposits. Andy is too sex-wasted to care. One spasm after another wracks my body. When it's over, I collapse down onto the couch beside him.

After a few seconds Andy turns and looks at me. "Do all queers suck cock like that?" he asks in amazement.

I laugh. "Some are better at it than others," I say. "Today I was particularly inspired."

I get up, get a towel, and toss it to Andy. He wipes his face and torso thoughtfully. He gets up and pulls his clothes on. I give him one of my T-shirts to make up for the one I tore off. While he's slipping it on, I scoop the five twenties off the table and hand them to him.

"Thanks," I say. "You more than earned it." Andy takes the money without saying anything, and stuffs it in his front pants pocket. He avoids looking in my eyes.

I walk him to the door. Finally, he raises his head and looks at me. "Um, listen," he says. "I been seeing this girl, we're like pretty tight. Only she's Catholic." He gives an embarrassed laugh. "You know how Catholic girls are." He shrugs. "Well, maybe you don't. They don't put out."

Why is he telling me this? I wonder. "Is this Angela you're talking about?" I ask.

Andy glances at his tattoo and laughs. "Hell, no. Me and Angela broke up almost a year ago." He shakes his head. "That tattoo was a dumb idea." He clears his throat. "Anyway, sometimes I get so frustrated I feel like I'm about to bust a nut." To my amazement, Andy turns bright red. He stands there, obviously struggling to go on.

"And . . . ?" I prompt.

"And," Andy blurts, "I was wondering if maybe we could do this again some time." The words are tumbling out now. "You wouldn't have to pay me or nothin'. Just some time, maybe, after I've been with my girlfriend and she goes through that 'Not till we're married' bullshit again, I could come over here and you could do what you did today." He shakes his head. "Jeez, I ain't *never* been blown like that. I didn't know a blow job could feel that good."

"Andy," I say. "You got yourself a deal." I hold out my hand. Embarrassed, Andy shakes it and then quickly lets go.

"Okay, well I gotta go," Andy mumbles. He opens the door and walks out into the apartment hallway. He turns to me and gives me a small smile. "Bye."

I smile back. "Bye."

I close the door. *Fuckin' amazing*, I think. Andy's old torn T-shirt is on the floor. I pick it up, bury my face in it, and take a long whiff. I walk into my bedroom and carefully place it in my top dresser drawer.

DAD'S PORNO BOY

T HE FIRST thing I think of when I wake up this morning, even
before my eyes have opened, is my phone conversation with
Richard last night. There I am, lying in bed, with Sonny and Cher
singing "I Got You, Babe" on the clock radio, and instead of getting up and getting ready for work like I'm supposed to, I'm just
rehashing the news Richard dropped on me. I can't believe he's
dropped out of college. For six months now! All this time I'm
thinking he's back at U.C. Berkeley studying engineering, prepar-
ing himself for a steady, well-paying career, and he's been screwing
around doing God knows what. He certainly wasn't about to tell
me.

I drag my sorry butt out of bed, strip and step into the shower.
I slept lousy last night, and the sting of cold water against my face
gives me the shock I need to wake up. I turn the shower nozzle to
hot and just let the water stream down my body for a good, long
time.

Afterwards, I wipe clean the bathroom mirror and shave. The
face that looks back at me is a little bleary-eyed, but still, for a man
who's going to turn forty in a couple of months, I don't have much
to complain about. There's a little gray around the temples, but
the hair's still thick. The few lines in the face just make me look
rugged. Today, more than usual, I see Richard staring back at me:
the same dark brown eyes, the same square jaw with the cleft in
it, the same bushy eyebrows. There's nothing of his mother in him;
sometimes I feel like he's more of a clone than a natural son.
Whatever, I certainly don't remember ever giving my old man the
grief that Richard gives me.

On the train into work, I see a young man sitting across the
aisle, reading the Times. He can't be much older than Richard,
mid-twenties at most. He's dressed in a blue, pin-striped suit, his
hair cut stylishly, very dapper looking. Probably has a job somewhere in the financial district, maybe in one of the law firms there,
or the banks. A young man with a future to him. What the hell

is Richard going to do without a college education, deliver pizzas? I keep looking at the man, wondering about him. Actually, he's not a bad looking guy, dark, with good strong features. He wears his suit well, and I'm willing to bet that he works out, that his body is in good shape, toned. I visualize him naked, and, for the hell of it, imagine his cock to be thick and meaty, his balls hanging low and ripe. I feel my own dick stir, and I let the fantasies take on a life of their own, imagining what it would be like to plow his young, corporate ass. He glances up at his paper and our eyes meet. His eyes are slate blue and steady, the eyes of a confident man who knows where he's going. I quickly shift my gaze out the window and watch the tract houses whiz by in the dim morning light.

By the time I walk through the office doors I'm thoroughly depressed. I grab a cup of coffee from the lobby canteen and quickly make my way to the privacy of my cubicle, avoiding all contact with co-workers. I just don't have it in me to muster up any small talk right now. My in-basket is full and I have two reports and a memo to crank out, not to mention a couple of briefings to prepare for, but I just sit back and slowly sip my coffee. I push down a sudden strong urge for a cigarette, like I haven't felt since I gave them up six years ago. I glance at the picture of Richard on my desk. It was taken last year, when he was on the Berkeley swim team. He's in his Speedos, poised on the edge of a pool, his knees bent, his arms pulled back, his face a study of concentration. What a handsome kid, I think. My beautiful son, Richard. For a second I feel like I'm going to cry.

All that morning I try to concentrate on my work, but it's hopeless. I know what I've got to do, the one thing that always lifts my spirits, and I just count the minutes till lunchtime rolls around. A little before noon, a couple of the guys come by and ask if I want to join them for sushi, but I say no, I got other plans. I spray a couple of squirts of Binaca in my mouth, comb my hair and adjust my tie, and get my ass out of that office as fast as I can. I can feel my mood lighten up as soon as I hit the streets. In fact, I'm feeling pretty excited now. I push through the downtown lunch crowds at a quick, don't-fuck-with-me trot.

After a while the crowds start thinning out. The downtown restaurants and shops give way to greasy-spoons, liquor stores, and vacant, boarded-up shop fronts. The sidewalks are dirty and covered with litter, and every now and then I have to step over the legs of some wino passed out in a doorway. People I pass take in my businessman's suit and give me the fish eye, or else ask me for money. Or both. Along with my excitement is a good dose of uneasiness. I remind myself that I've been in this neighborhood many times before without getting my brains blown out by some crackhead. But it's a relief when I finally see the blinking sign of Frenchy's Video Palace and can get in off the streets.

There are a few men hanging around the magazine racks, leafing through the pictures, but that's not where my interests lie. I walk up to the counter, slap down a ten dollar bill and get a pile of tokens. Already I've got a hard-on the size of Florida, and I'm not even back where the good stuff is. I stroll into the arcade.

There's a good crowd there today. Guys line the passageway, leaning against the booth doors. All eyes turn to me as I walk in, checking out what the new meat looks like. The place is a dump, grimy and beat-up, the booths smelling of piss and Lysol. Instead of being a turn-off, the whole sleazy set-up excites the hell out of me. I feel very cocky right now. I'm a good-looking guy and I've rarely had trouble scaring up a little action whenever I wanted it. Granted, I must look a little ridiculous in my Italian suit. However, it's cut well and shows off my body nicely, the wide shoulders and narrow hips, and I hope it's feeding into some corporate daddy fantasy that some of the younger guys here might be having.

I walk slowly down the aisle, scanning the crowd. There are some possibilities here: a blond, tough-looking kid in jeans and a Giants T-shirt (probably hustling); some bearded bear, husky but not fat, with a chest full of hair sprouting out above the top button of his flannel shirt; a dude in a Levi jacket and black chino pants, wearing shades (I get a picture of him stumbling and groping his way down the aisle to his present spot. It's hard enough to see in here without wearing sunglasses, for Christ's sake). I look closer at the last guy. I can't see his eyes, but by the tilt of his head, I know he's checking me out as well.

I turn the corner, and there's the man I know I want to make it with. He's leaning against the wall, arms crossed against his chest, watching the scene with a cool, unreadable expression. My eyes scan down his body, taking in the short-cropped red hair, the narrowed eyes, the pumped up biceps (the left one encircled by a barbed wire tattoo). The tank top he's wearing is tight enough to show a well-muscled, lean torso, the nipples etched against the fabric. His jeans are torn and frayed at the basket, and the shit-kickers he's got on are beat-up and scruffy. A real urban cowboy. He's fucking beautiful, and my dick gives a throb just looking at him. Our eyes meet, and I hold the glance long enough to let him know I'm interested. He doesn't look away but his face isn't giving me any clues either about what he's thinking. I'm the one that breaks eye contact, suddenly uneasy. That's a shock. I'm usually never nervous in these encounters. After a while I sneak another glance at him and see him still looking me over. He gives a slight nod.

We happen to be back where the buddy booths are. I go into one, heart pounding, drop a few tokens in the slot, and wait. I absently watch the suck-and-fuck drama on the screen, wondering if the dude's going to give me a tumble. After a few seconds, I hear the door open and shut in the booth next to mine.

I let a few more seconds go by and then push the buddy booth button. The opaque wall separating the booths goes clear, and there's the guy, with his jeans down around his ankles, stroking his dick, his balls tight and plump underneath. His face is more relaxed now, more animated, and his wide, strong mouth curves upward into a faint smile. His eyes once more lock onto mine, and we eye-fuck each other as his hand slowly slides up and down that meaty cock of his. He lets go of his dick and peels his tank top off. His body is tight and smooth, his chest lightly freckled, his nipples wide and copper colored. He reaches up and squeezes them between the thumb and forefinger of each hand, swaying his hips from side to side. I watch that heavy meat of his swing slowly between his thighs, wondering what it must taste like full down my throat. The dude turns around and shows me an ass that is perfection, smooth and firm, the back of his thighs bunched with muscles. I can't begin to guess how many squats at the weight bar he must do every week to get thighs like that. He could crack walnuts with those thighs.

He turns again and faces me. There's an expectant look on his face. I guess it's my turn to show my stuff, which I'm quite willing to do. I proceed to do a businessman's strip for him, pulling off my tie, taking my jacket off and laying it carefully on the seat (God forbid it should fall onto the floor of this booth; I'd probably have to burn it afterwards). I unbutton my shirt buttons, starting from the top and slip my shirt off. Regular workouts at the company gym have given me a nicely pumped body which I'm only too happy to show. My torso is darker and hairier than his, not as defined, but sturdier. I drop my pants and then slowly draw down my boxers. Liberated, my dick springs to full attention. The guy's got his eyes fixed hard on it, checking it out. I know the expression he's wearing well. Dick hunger. I wrap my palm around my dickmeat and stroke, first slow, then faster, my balls bouncing hard to the rhythm of my hand. The dude's stroking his own meat again and we stand there for a couple of minutes, fucking our hands, showing what we got to each other. He comes right up to the window and humps the glass. I watch his thick meat pressed against the window, sliding up and down it, leaving a smear of pre-cum on it.

It's time to move on up to the real thing. I motion to him to come join me in my booth and he nods okay. He pulls his pants back on and a few seconds later we're together in my booth, nice and cozy. I drop the rest of my tokens into the slot to keep the video going indefinitely. I smile at him.

"Hi," I say.

He smiles back. "Howdy." He runs his hands across my torso, flicking my nipples with his thumbs. He leans over and lightly runs his tongue over them, then nips the right one gently between his teeth.

"Jesus, that feels good," I groan. His grin widens. He's got a friendly, boyish smile that goes counter to the tough guy image he gave off outside. He leans over and kisses me lightly. I open my mouth and he slips his tongue in, damn near down my throat. I return the favor, frenching him hard as my hands wander over his torso. I slide my hands into the back pockets of his jeans and pull his body tight against me, dry-humping his jeans with my stiff dick. He reaches down and cups my balls, squeezing them gently.

He pulls back a little and his eyes meet mine. "What's your name?"

I give a slight laugh. "Does it matter?"

"Yeah. I don't fuck strangers."

How quaint, I think. But I'm willing to play along. "I'm Chris," I say.

He smiles. "Is that your real name or are you making one up?"

I laugh. "I never lie to a man who's got my balls in his hand."

He laughs too. "I'm Steve."

"Well, Steve," I say. "Now that we got the introductions over with, do you mind if I suck your cock for a while?"

Steve shrugs and grins. "Go for it," he says.

I sit on the booth's seat, my hands on Steve's hips and pull him close. I unzip his jeans and tug them down. In the dim light from the video screen I examine his cock, taking in the meaty hang of it, tracing the one big vein up the shaft, how the piss slit peeks out from his uncut foreskin. I breathe in the musky smell of his dick and balls, a scent I could get drunk on. His balls hang tight against his body, each nut plump in the sac, filled with his sweet jizz. I pull the foreskin over his cockhead, and then begin to stroke his dickmeat slowly. It's warm in my hand and has a nice, solid heft to it. Steve twitches it and it feels like something with a life of its own. I squeeze the thick tube of flesh and a drop of pre-cum oozes out.

I slowly run my tongue up the length of his dick and twirl it around its head. My hands slide across his hips and over his ass. I grab a hold of both ass cheeks and pull him close to me, sliding my mouth down his dick until my nose buries itself into his pubes. I keep his cock shoved all the way down my throat for a full half minute, my tongue doing the slip-slide around the thick shaft. Steve sighs and begins pumping his hips. I twist my head from side to side to increase the sensation of my lips sliding along his dick-meat and Steve groans his appreciation. I look up at Steve, his dick still crammed deep down my throat. Our eyes meet, and Steve flashes me his "aw-shucks" smile again. *Christ*, I think. *I feel like I'm giving Huckleberry Finn a blow job.* Steve pumps my mouth with long slow strokes, and each time I take the meaty shaft in up to the base. My hands slide up his hard torso until I reach his nipples. I squeeze each one, not gently, and feel his whole body shudder.

A few moments of this and Steve suddenly pulls his dick out of my mouth. When I lean forward to swallow it again, he pulls away. "Wait a second," he gasps. After a beat he grins. "Whew.

I almost shot a load then, and I'm enjoying this too much to end it so soon." I tongue his balls for a while, and then swallow them both in my mouth.

"Yeah," he sighs. "Look at that hot man suck on my nuts." He reaches down and pulls me up. "I think it's time for me to eat dick for a while."

Who am I to argue with the man? I stand up and Steve takes my place on the seat. For a few seconds he just stares at my dick, taking it in with his eyes. My meat rests against my thigh, half hard. "Fucking beautiful," he murmurs. He wraps his palm around it and strokes it a few times to get me to full erection. He succeeds. Damn, it feels nice to have another man's hand around my dick. It's been too long.

Steve runs his tongue up and down my balls, bathing them carefully. He nuzzles under my nut sac, tonguing the hairy path to my asshole and back to my balls again. He slides his mouth down my dick shaft, sucking on my meat, running his tongue over it. The sensations are indescribable. My hands run through his short hair and alongside his temples, guiding his head back and forth as I fuck his face. We achieve a certain rhythm, Steve descending down onto my dickmeat as I thrust full into his mouth. I watch my dick pump in and out of this handsome young man's eager mouth, and that sight alone is enough to make me want to squirt a load. I feel Steve's hands pry apart my ass cheeks and it isn't long before he works a finger up my bunghole. He finger fucks me leisurely, squirming his digit deep into my ass. I groan loudly, but quickly stifle it, biting down on my lower lip. Jolts of pleasure sweep over me and my legs begin to tremble. It's too soon to cum; like Steve I want to drag this out. I close my eyes and count my breaths, a trick I use whenever I want to keep from shooting. I open my eyes again and glance at the sex video playing on the screen. And see Richard looking back at me.

My body stiffens. Steve looks up at me. "Did I use my teeth?" he asks.

"No, no," I say distractedly. "You're doing great. Please don't stop."

Steve shoots me a half-quizzical look but is only too happy to go on eating dick.

I look back at the video. At first I think that my eyes must have been playing tricks on me, that I got Richard too much on my mind and this is just some actor that *looks* like him. But it only takes me a couple of seconds to convince myself that this is in fact my son looking back at the camera, stretched out on a bed, stroking his dick. My first thought is *well, at least he's not delivering pizzas*, and I almost laugh, more out of shock than anything else.

It doesn't take long for the shock to give way to fury. *So this is what Richard gave college up for*, I think. *That damn fool kid! What the hell was he thinking!*

Part of me wants to just get the hell out of the booth and try to figure out how I'm going to deal with this. But I stay put, still letting Steve work over my dick and ass as I watch the video. I can't tear myself away. I have never seen Richard naked before, at least not as a grown man, and I find it perversely fascinating to watch him. His swimmer's build is heavier now, more muscular, the abs and pecs more sharply defined. It's obvious he's been working out in a gym. In a way, it's like watching a video of me as a young man. Richard smiles at the camera, and I recognize my smile; I've seen it in the mirror hundreds of times. I see myself in Richard's eyes, his coloring, his mouth, his build. Christ, even his dick is mine! The same curve to the left, the same flared head, the same thick, veined shaft. His balls hang low, the right one lower than the left, just like mine.

Another man enters into the camera's range, blonde, well-built, about Richard's age. And equally naked. They wrestle around on the bed, and it's only a few moments before he goes down on Richard, sucking Richard's dick with long, wet strokes. I'm watching all this, watching my son get blown on video while my own dick is getting sucked by Huck Finn. My brain buzzes with unreality.

It doesn't take long before Richard is fucking the other guy's ass. They're both stretched out on the bed, Richard lying behind, his arms wrapped around the blonde man's hairless torso. He pumps his hips with an easy, slow rhythm, driving his dick hard up the other's ass. Richard's eyes are narrowed in concentration, an expression so familiar to me I can trace it back to the crib. It's the same expression he wears in the photo on my desk. Yet he's grinning, too, obviously enjoying himself. The kid's got star quality, there's no denying it.

It's gotten almost unbearably hot in this booth. Perspiration runs down my forehead into my eyes, my torso is drenched, and I can feel a trickle of sweat work its way down my back into the crack of my ass. Steve's finger massages my prostate, working my ass in such a way that the pleasure is almost too painful to bear. Richard has rolled over on his back and his partner rides Richard's dick astride his torso, facing the camera. All I can see of Richard is his muscular hairy legs, his balls, now drawn up tight against his body, and the shaft of his dick thrusting in and out of the other man's hole. A camera shot to Richard's face shows him panting heavily, his mouth open, his eyes glassy and wide. He pulls his dick out of the other man's ass and starts beating off, his body arched, his balls bouncing furiously. I whip my dick out of Steve's mouth and do the same, matching Richard stroke for stroke. We both shoot at the same time, my load blasting out of my dick onto Steve's face the same time that Richard's wad splatters against the belly of his partner. I look down and see Steve shooting his load into his hand, the cum dripping out between his fingers. I collapse against the wall, panting.

Steve stands up, pulling his pants up with him. His dick hangs out of his fly as he pulls out a handkerchief and wipes his face. "That sure was a hell of a lot of fun," he grins.

I make a grunt of agreement and try to return his smile. But I can't stop watching the video. I may be just about drained for the time being, but Richard is hard again and plowing ass like there's hell to pay. Just like me, at his age.

Steve follows my gaze and glances at the video. "Hot man," he comments, looking at Richard. His eyes shift towards me, towards the video again, and back again at me. "He looks like you," he says.

"You think so?" I ask absently. I put my clothes back on. My suit is a rumpled mess. Thank God I don't have any meetings this afternoon. I feel dazed and weak, and all I want to do is get out of that damn booth. When I finish dressing I shake Steve's hand. "Thanks," I say. "We'll have to do this again some time." Steve looks a little taken aback. It's only when I'm in the front part of the store that I realize how stupid I must have sounded, like Steve and I had just taken in a movie. I almost laugh out loud at that thought. In a way, we did just that.

At the counter by the door I see a video box with Richard's picture on it, smiling his easy smile back out at the world at large. Richard always has been big on charm. I can see why he would be a natural at this. I get the clerk's attention and nod at the box.

"How much is that video?" I ask him.

The clerk tells me it's $69 plus tax. I hand him my charge card and he writes it up. As I walk out, I put the video in my inner coat pocket. It would not be a good idea to be seen carrying it into the office. I wonder what it will be like tonight, watching this video again in the privacy of my own apartment. Maybe jerking off to it. I glance at my watch and see that I'm late. A light turns yellow and I run hard across the street. Some jerk honks at me, but I got more important things on my mind than to be bothered by that. I move through the crowds as fast as I can, wondering what the hell I'm going to say to Richard next time I talk to him.

FIREMAN NICK SLIDES THE POLE

FIRE MAKES MY dick hard. Something about flames shooting up
into the sky, roaring, timbers cracking, buildings caving in under an explosion of sparks and smoke. . . . I can't begin to tell you
how much a scene like that makes me want to squirt a load. If
there had been just one little extra twist in my psyche, I could have
been a raving pyromaniac, torching buildings and jerking off in
some dark alley across the street as they go up in flames. Instead,
I'm a decent, law-abiding guy who would never jeopardize anybody's life or property. It's just not in me. So my fascination has
taken another channel. I'm a fireman.

*　*　*

I'm awakened out of my sleep by the loud clanging of the
alarms, and I'm fully dressed and sliding down the pole before my
mind has even registered that I'm out of bed. This is a three
alarmer, a biggie, and I'm raring to go. I'm still a Johnnie, a new
guy, I've been on the force for a little less than a year, and I'm
about to lose my three alarm cherry tonight. I sit in the tiller seat,
tugging on the rear steering wheel as the engine goes tearing down
the city streets with sirens wailing, and all I can think is *this sure
as hell beats Disneyland.*

Even a mile away I can see a glow in the night sky ahead of us,
and a little later a huge mushroom cloud, just as if someone had
nuked the neighborhood. A few minutes later we come to a
screaming halt and leap out of the fire engine. I take in the scene
while on a full run. The upper stories of an apartment building
are in flames and smoke pours out from the roof in black billows.
All the top story windows blaze with red light; it's as if the tenants
were all up and throwing a party. The flames roar so loud the
sound just rolls over me like waves, and I can feel the heat pound
down on me like a concussion. Hot damn, is this a kick in the ass
or what! I'm so horny I could hump the first thing on two legs that
comes my way!

We look for an empty hydrant to connect to, not an easy task since there are already two other engines ahead of us, hooked up with their firemen holding onto their hoses and spewing water. The searchlight units are in full operation, and the whole scene looks like a Hollywood set. My partner, Tom, and I put on our breathing apparatus, grab our equipment, and run into the building.

We race up the stairs, shoving past a stream of bewildered tenants clutching blankets and screaming like the damned as they flee towards the lobby. On the sixth floor the smoke pours down the corridor. As prearranged, Tom goes one way, I go the other, busting down doors with our fire axes, making sure all the living units have been evacuated. I swing my ax against the doors like Thor, the friggin' thunder god, and each time I hear the wood splinter, my dick just gets a little harder.

I do this for three separate units with nothing to show for it; they've all been vacated. That leaves one more unit at the end of the corridor. Smoke is pouring down from cracks in the ceiling tiles; the fire must be directly overhead now. If I were playing this by the book, I'd get my ass out of there *now;* in a couple of minutes the whole damn ceiling is going to come down. But I go ahead and smash the door down in three swings and dive into the apartment.

It's like diving into black ink. I'm going by feel alone here. Carpet under my feet, a sofa, I must be in the living room. Now I'm on linoleum, this must be the kitchen. I find another door, push in to the next room, stumble, and fall. It takes a few seconds before I realize I've tripped over a body, sprawled on the floor, bed sheets still tangled around the legs. At the same moment I hear a muffled crash as the outside corridor ceiling collapses. There's no going back now.

The adrenalin is racing through me. I heave the body over my shoulders, stumble across the room until I find the windows, and smash them open with my ax. With the rush of air, the fire flares up, illuminating everything. I get a glimpse of a dangling arm and the naked torso of the body slung around my neck, but I can't see the face. There's a fire escape outside and I clamber onto it. I lumber down as best I can, the flames giving me one final goose before I'm below the range of fire. It's only when I'm in the courtyard itself that I feel safe. I ease the body down, rip my mask off, and by the light of the flames above check out just who the hell I've been carrying.

It's a man, buck naked, either unconscious or dead, I can't tell. He lies sprawled on his back, unmoving, and it only takes me a second to see he's not breathing. I check his carotid artery for a pulse and finally find one, weak and fluttering. I drop to my knees, lift his chin up, cover his mouth with mine, and blow hard. His chest rises and falls once. I keep on breathing into his mouth, timing myself, twelve breaths per minute. I take half a second to look around. I'm in some inner courtyard, completely alone with this guy. Everyone else must be in front, fighting the fire. *Where the fuck are the paramedics?* I wonder. I can still hear the flames crackling overhead and burning sparks fly all around me. I check to see if the guy's breathing on his own. He's not. I continue the resuscitation.

It takes about ten minutes before he finally starts breathing raggedly. He coughs and it's the most beautiful sound I've ever heard. I feel a thrill of excitement. *I did it!* I think. *I brought the motherfucker back to life!* I feel like God! The man lies there gasping and wheezing, and for the first time I take the opportunity to really look at him. I'm startled to see how *young* he is, barely out of his teens. His body is smooth and firm, and as I stare at him in the ruddy light of the fire, all I can think of is how *beautiful* he looks.

His breathing is still shallow and erratic. I plant my mouth over his again and continue to breathe life into him. My left hand lies lightly on his chest, above his nipple. Without thinking, I take the nipple between my thumb and forefinger and squeeze, while my tongue slips into his mouth. His body stirs and he bends his left leg up. My hand crosses his chest and tenderly pinches the other nipple. He groans. I look down the length of his body and see his cock is rock hard. "Hallelujah!" I laugh. "He has risen!" I bend over and french him for all I'm worth as my hand slips down and circles his fat, soot-stained cock.

His tongue pushes into my mouth now. "Oh, yeah, Susan," he murmurs. I pull back. His eyes flutter open and he stares with dilated pupils into the night sky. "Susan?" he murmurs again, his voice stronger. I quickly let go of his cock. He turns his head towards me. His eyes focus with difficulty and I can see the jolt of shock pass over his face as he takes me in. "Wha . . . ?" he exclaims, trying to get up.

"Easy," I murmur, gently pushing him back onto the pavement. "Lie still. I just pulled you out of the fire." Hopefully he'll think that everything that just happened was a near-death hallucination. I look up and see Tom in the courtyard entrance, staring at us. God know how long he's been there or how much he's seen.

"Where are the paramedics?" I holler. "This guy needs medical attention *now!*"

Tom turns his head to the darkness behind him. "Over here!" he shouts. I hear a trample of feet and a team of paramedics bursts into the courtyard. It takes them less than a second to appraise the situation, and it's only a matter of moments more before they're carting the man off on a stretcher, an oxygen mask over his mouth.

"Good work, Nick!" one of them calls over to me as they exit the courtyard. "It looks like he's going to make it!"

I follow them out to the ambulance. There's a camera crew from a local news station filming us as we approach. As I pass Tom, I nod and grin. He looks back at me, but says nothing, his eyes quizzical. *Just how much did he see?* I wonder.

* * *

The first thing I do back in the station house is strip and jump in the shower. Mike and Lenny, two other guys on my team, are already in there, soaped up and scrubbing the soot off. Mike's good-natured Irish face breaks into a grin as I walk in.

"Hey, it's the local hero!" he cries out. "The kid's first three-alarm fire and he hogs all the glory!"

Lenny slaps a soapy hand against my back. "You're quite the star, Nick, saving that guy's life. How're you feeling?"

I give an aw-shucks smile and grunt politely. But the adrenalin is still pumping fast within me. I keep remembering the heat of the flames, the explosion of sparks, me playing dueling tongues with that hot naked guy in the courtyard. *I'm hornier than a motherfucker, is how I'm feeling, Lenny,* I think. I look at Mike's tight, smooth body, his beefy Irish cock crowned by a flaming red pubic bush, and it's all I can do to keep from dropping to my knees and swallowing it down to the last inch. Lenny turns his back to me as he soaps down his chest. I sneak a glimpse of his perfect, nut-brown ass and wonder what it would feel like to plow it home. I feel my dick growing hard and I have to close my eyes and think of baseball statistics to keep it soft.

Tom walks in and my dick springs back to life immediately. I have to turn my back on all of them and recite in my mind "The Wreck of the Hesperus" before my meat behaves itself again. I have always had a hard-on for Tom. He's such a straight-arrow: his dark blonde hair is always cut short and per the regulations, his moustache clipped neatly, his uniform always starched and pressed. He is so damned *earnest*. And yet he's the sweetest guy in the world, true-blue and serious, rock-solid and utterly depend-able. Maybe he makes my gonads churn so much because he's so completely the opposite of me. And of course because he's fuckin' gorgeous, with a solid, muscular body, a face off of a recruitment poster, and a fat, meaty dick that is now swinging between his thighs like the bells of Notre Dame.

Lenny turns off his shower and walks out. Mike does the same. Now it's just me and Tom alone in the fire station shower room at three o'clock in the morning. All of a sudden the atmosphere gets *very* heavy in here. I sneak a glance at Tom and catch him looking at me. He quickly looks away.

I clear my throat. "Some fire, huh?" I say cheerfully.

Tom shrugs and mumbles something. There's another awkward moment. I'm not exactly enjoying this, but all this *drama* is kind of funny; it's like a scene from a bad movie. Played naked. At least Tom's embarrassment gives me the chance to sneak a few, linger-ing looks at his thick, uncut tool. My gaze quickly shifts up to his face as he turns and confronts me, a troubled look in his beauti-ful slate-gray eyes.

"Nick, I got to clear this up," he says, his voice ragged. "What the hell were you doing to that guy in the courtyard?"

I give Tom my best poker face. "I believe it's called mouth-to-mouth resuscitation, Tom," I say calmly.

"Yeah, right!" Tom snarls. Now this surprises me. I have never seen Tom snarl. I didn't even know he *could* snarl.

"Is something upsetting you, Tom?" I ask in the same calm tone. Even though I like Tom, I can't help baiting him.

"Christ, you must take me for a fucking idiot!" Tom explodes. "I saw what you were doing with that guy! You were practically humping him! What a fucking asshole, unprofessional thing to do!" This from a guy who before tonight I've never heard say anything worse than "damn." Tom's face is beet red now, and a vein in his forehead is throbbing dangerously. He's pacing back and forth under the shower. "I ought to fuckin' turn you in." His lip curls up into a sneer. "Mr. Hero. Mr. Big Shot. What a joke!"

Old Tom's got a major hair up his ass about something, I think. I'm finding all this righteous indignation a little hard to believe. I'm not a sadistic guy by nature, but I feel an overwhelming curiosity to push this and see what happens. I stand there looking at Tom with my arms crossed against my chest and let my dick get hard. I give him my nastiest grin. "What's the matter, Tom?" I leer. "You feeling a little jealous you weren't in on the action?"

That does the trick all right. "Why you son-of-a-bitch," Tom growls. He crosses the shower room in three steps with fists cocked and swings at me. I duck but don't hit back, even though he's left his right flank exposed for a clear shot. This just enrages Tom more. He throws a body tackle on me, arms wrapped around my waist, and we both go down on the tile floor. We roll around, the water hissing on us from the shower nozzles above. I swing over on top of him and for an instant I look down full into Tom's eyes. Instead of the rage I expected, I see fear. And beneath that, something else. Excitement.

Tom pushes me off and wraps his arms around me in a tight bear hug. I'm a strong guy, but I can't break free and I feel the air squeezed out of me. Tom's face is no more than an inch away from mine. I quit struggling. "Come on, fight, you bastard," Tom snarls. I laugh, a little wheezingly, I confess. Tom looks startled, and I quickly take the opportunity to raise my head and plant a big wet kiss full on his lips. His mouth falls open in surprise, and I push my tongue in deep, frenching him for all that I'm worth. Tom tries to pull away, but this time I'm the one who holds on tight. I grind my pelvis against Tom's and dry hump his hard belly. The blood sings in my ears. It's the burning building all over again, the fire and smoke, the rain of sparks, the excitement!

Tom fights hard, and then suddenly he stops. It takes a second for me to realize that he's kissing me back. His tongue shoves deep into my mouth and his hands are suddenly all over me, sliding along my torso, kneading the flesh. They move down, cup my ass cheeks and squeeze hard; I feel his stiff cock thrust urgently against my abdomen.

Tom is just full of surprises tonight, but I'm quick to shift gears. We roll around on the tile floor, our mouths fused together, dry humping each other like a couple of dogs in heat. I reach down and start stroking Tom's thick dick; the way it fills my palm promises some hot times ahead. I lift his arm and bury my face into his pit; I feel Tom's tongue burrow deep into my ear.

Tom straddles my torso and pins my arms down. He looks down at me, panting, the water plastering his hair against his skull. Without taking his eyes off of my face, he reaches up behind him and turns the shower off. There's a crazed look in his eyes that probably should make me a little nervous. It doesn't. Something in Tom is busting out and I'm willing to push this for all it's worth. He grinds his pelvis against mine and our cocks slap together. I wrap my hand around both of them and stroke them, cock flesh squirming against cock flesh. Tom grins, bends down, and we kiss, long and hard, sucking on each other's tongues, as we both fuck my fist.

Tom pulls away and sits up straight again; I take the opportunity to really drink him in. My eyes travel down from his handsome face to the muscular, smooth torso, dusted lightly with dark blonde hair. His nipples are dark pink and wide; I reach up and brush my thumbs against them, before tweaking them hard. Tom groans. I take in his abs, beautifully chiselled into a sharply defined six-pack, an appendix scar highlighting their perfection. Beneath his dark pubic bush, his dickmeat juts out impressively, red and blood engorged. It's the first time I've seen Tom's dick hard and I savor the moment. I trace the veins that run up the meaty shaft, see how the knob of his cockhead flares out from the uncut foreskin. His ball sac hangs high and tight, the two plump nuts swelling up inside, begging to be licked.

It's a request I can't refuse. "Slide down," I growl, and Tom is only too happy to comply. He squirms down my torso until his knees pin my shoulders, and he drops his balls in my mouth. I give them a good, thorough washing, rolling them around gently with my tongue, sucking on the sac. Tom slaps my face with his dickmeat, rubbing it over my cheeks, my eyes, my nose. I look up and our eyes meet. Tom grins. "Yeah, Nick," he growls. "Suck on those nuts. Get all the soot off."

A few seconds later, I release his balls; my tongue travels down the hairy, dark path to his asshole. Tom shifts his body again and sits square on my face. I feel his fleshy ass cheeks press down on me, burying my nose and mouth, and my tongue probes the crack until it finds the juicy bunghole. I shove my tongue up against the sphincter and give his ass a good working over. By the way Tom squirms on my face, I can tell he's just having a grand old time.

Tom lifts his leg and swings his body around. He buries his face into my crotch and starts a feeding frenzy, eating my ass, sucking on my balls, sliding his tongue up and down my dick shaft. There's a pause and then I feel him take my meat in his mouth and, with exquisite slowness, swallow it down to the base. I give a loud groan that trails off into a deep sigh. *For a beginner, this guy is doing a damn good job.* I think. *He's a natural.* I start pumping my hips, plowing Tom's mouth with long, quick strokes. Tom's dick thrusts above me invitingly, and I raise my head and swallow it. We both work each other's mouths, fucking our faces enthusiastically, greedily feeding off of each other's dickmeat.

I work Tom's dick like the pro that I am. I take it all in, filling my mouth with it, letting my tongue squirm over the meaty shaft. Sucking hard, I slide my lips back up the thick meat, twisting my head from side to side for maximum effect. When my lips reach Tom's cockhead, I roll my tongue around it, and then work my lips down the shaft again, slowly, teasingly, with loud sucking noises. I'm a real pig when it comes to dick; I just can't get enough of the cock of a handsome man. I feel Tom's body squirm appreciatively, and it isn't long before he starts groaning loud enough to bounce echoes off the tile ceiling of the shower room. I just hope the guys in the fire station dorm are sleeping soundly tonight.

Tom reaches up to the soap dispenser and squirts a couple of dollops into the palm of his hand. He pries apart my ass cheeks and his finger works my bunghole, slipping it in up to the third joint. Sweet Jesus, does that ever feel good! He finger fucks me with short, vicious jabs that keep me gasping for more. "I would really like to shove my cock hard up your ass, Nick," he says earnestly, like he's asking me to go out to the movies with him.

"I want you to hold that thought, Tom," I grin. I scramble to my feet and run out into the locker room. There's a condom machine right by the shower room door. This is not the time to go fumbling for quarters; I give the machine three hard smacks with the heel of my hand, and a condom packet drops out of the slot (a trick I learned by my first week on the job). I rush back and toss the condom to Tom. "I take it you know how to use this," I say.

Tom grins. "Oh, yeah. Up to now, only to keep the ladies from getting pregnant. But I can adapt to the situation." He rolls the condom down his dick shaft, pushes me onto my back and hoists my legs over his shoulders. I feel his dickhead poke a couple of times against my hole and then slowly, with excruciating patience, he works his cock inside of me. I close my eyes and savor the sensation of being filled. When I open them again, his face is right above me, his lips pulled back into something between a snarl and a grin, his eyes fierce. Tom starts pumping his hips hard, punishing my ass with quick, savage strokes, daring me to take it.

Okay, Tom, I think. *You want to scrap? Let's scrap.* I wrap my legs tight around his torso and pivot him onto his back. Tom's face registers surprise. I clamp my ass muscles tight and meet him stroke for stroke, riding his cock like a cowboy on a bucking bronco. Tom gasps with the sudden pleasure. We roll around on the shower floor, wrestling and squirming against each other, hips pumping, bodies joined by Tom's thick meat hard up my ass. Tom wraps a soapy hand around my dick and slides it up and down. I reach down and twist his nipples hard. We're in a fierce competition to see who can weaken the other the most by pleasure. We both give as good as we get.

Tom's lips are open and his eyes are getting glassy. Groans trickle out of his mouth, each time getting a little longer and a little louder. I rhythmically loosen and tighten my sphincter as I ride him, quickening my pace, holding on to his muscular torso to steady myself. Tom shows no mercy as he pounds my ass, which is just the way I like it. I reach back behind and fill my hand with his balls. They're pulled up tight, now, ready to give up their load of creamy jizz. I give them a good squeeze as I slide down Tom's shaft.

That does the trick. I feel the spasms move through Tom's body with an almost seismic force and he cries out loudly. I quickly cover my mouth with his, and kiss him fiercely; this is the only thing that keeps him from waking the whole damn crew up and bringing them into the shower room on a run. Tom's load gushes out of his dickmeat and slams into the condom up my ass; I can feel each squirt distinctly. His hand slides slickly up and down my own dick and it's only a matter of seconds before I feel my own body shuddering. I close my eyes and think of burning buildings as I squirt my load, splattering Tom's face and torso with hot, thick spunk. I collapse on Tom, and after a while I kiss him again, licking my cum off his face. We lie together on the shower floor for a long time, holding each other. Eventually we sneak back to our bunks in the dorm.

*   *   *

That morning the whole team gathers around the TV and turns on the morning news to see what they say about the fire. There's a shot of the paramedics wheeling the guy I saved into the ambulance. The newscaster even mentions me by name.

Lenny laughs. "You won't have any problems getting laid after today, Nickie."

"You think so?" I ask, grinning. I glance at Tom and waggle my eyebrows. To my amazement, he blushes, but he manages to give a small grin back at me. I turn back to the TV and see another shot of the building up in flames. I can feel my dick get hard all over again.

FIRE STORM ORGY

I NEVER PLAN TO have sex with Nick in the firehouse; it just seems to happen. The first time was in the shower room at three a.m. after putting out a three alarm fire in an east-side apartment house. Then there was that early Saturday morning when Nick walked into the locker room and caught me polishing my boots; it wasn't more than five minutes later that I was plowing his ass in the alcove behind the condom machine. And the time right in the dorm, when Nick came over to my bed around midnight to discuss the duty roster and ended up giving me a blow job while all the other firemen around us were sawing wood.

The funny thing is I am not like this normally: taking risks and doing crazy things that could get my ass fired. I'm a solid, dependable, salt-of-the-earth kind of guy. There's just something about Nick, that wild gleam in those beautiful dark eyes, that cocky smile, that loose-limbed easy way he walks, just a hair's breadth shy of a strut . . . he lights a fire in me that just rages out of control. And it's only when I get to squirt my hose, either while slamming his sweet perfect ass or deep throating his handsome face, that I can finally put that fire out and get some peace of mind.

Anyway, I was in the firehouse locker room giving Nick a blow job when the five alarm bell rang; I already had a condom in my hand, waiting to slip it on. Startled, I took Nick's dick out of my mouth and stared up at him. He looked back at me, eyes wide and I almost burst out laughing. In the year that I've known Nick, I have *never* seen him show shock, even with buildings burning down around our heads and us smashing our way out side-by-side with our fire axes. But I can't blame him. In all the years I've been on the force, we have never had a five alarm fire before. Fires of that intensity are the stuff of legend.

I clambered to my feet, stuffing the condom in my back pocket, and Nick quickly pulled his pants up. Not a second too soon, as the other firemen on duty came bursting in from the dorm. Jake was the first one in. I grabbed a hold of his arm as he rushed by.

"What the hell is going on?" I asked, shouting above the sudden din of the other voices and the sound of locker doors slamming.

Jake's eyes still had the half-focussed look of a man suddenly roused from sleep. "I don't know for sure," he replied. "All I heard was that the hills outside the city are all up in flames." He yanked his arm free and ripped open his locker door to get his gear.

Nick and I exchanged quick glances and right away I could see the excited gleam in his eye. I scrambled through the crowd of men to my locker and started pulling my own equipment out. As I tugged my coat on, I snuck another worried look Nick's way. He was getting his gear out too, his fingers zipping up his suit and strapping on his helmet with a quick, efficient economy of movement. Once again his eyes met mine. The only other times I've seen his face like that was when he was plowing my ass and working himself up to a bodacious orgasm. *Shit!* I thought. *I bet Nick's dick is rock hard now!* That was the problem with Nick. He was too fuckin' crazy to be in this line of work; in spite of his skill, it made him dangerous. For me, fighting fires was a way to make a living. For Nick, it was a goddamn religious experience, something as good as sex. Maybe better. He had this *thing* about fire that was more than a little wacko. It made him take risks that no fireman had any business taking.

In a matter of minutes we were on the fire engine, heading for the city outskirts, sirens screaming. Even though it was early morning, the sky was surprisingly dark, like a storm was rolling in. I looked up at Nick in the tiller seat. "Maybe we'll get lucky and get some rain," I shouted up to him.

He rolled his eyes. "Guess again, Tom," he shouted back.

I checked out the sky again and saw what he meant. Those weren't rainclouds for chrissake. That was *smoke*, like I've never seen it before, blowing in from the east, plunging the city into darkness. My eyes scanned the direction it was coming from. All I saw was blackness, churning out into the eastern horizon. For a second I saw a flicker of red light that must have been flame, but then it was lost again behind that curtain of smoke. *Holy shit!* I thought. *Are we ever in for it today!*

The police had cordoned off the roads leading up to the hills, and we slowed down as we made our way past the barricades and the mobs of people pressing against them. Things weren't any calmer on the other side of the police line; the area had become a war zone. Cars were careening down the narrow streets from the hills above, weaving dangerously among streams of running people clutching pets and possessions in their arms.

We got as far up the hill as the Claremont Hotel. Smoke swirled around its white Victorian towers, but it was coming from farther up the hill, and from the north. At least for now the hotel didn't seem to be in any immediate danger. A base of operations had been established in the parking lot. Other engines had pulled up into it, and there were uniforms everywhere, firemen to be sure, but also cops and even some National Guard.

Chavez, who was up front driving, pulled to a stop and we all jumped off. I recognized Chief McCabe over by the far end of the lot, already talking to two teams of firemen. He saw us and motioned us over to him. "The fire is sweeping down towards Grizzly Peak Boulevard," he shouted at us over the noise of the crowd. "We got two pumper trucks up there already, and the last I heard we still have pressure in the water mains. We've already made a couple of sweeps through the area with a bullhorn, telling people to evacuate, but there are still some damn fools up there trying to save their homes. I want you guys to do what you can to keep the fire from jumping the boulevard. And for God's sake, tell any civilians you see to get the hell out of there!"

"Okay, men," Chavez barked. "You heard him. Let's move!" We raced back to the truck and piled on. Chavez activated the siren and we roared up the hillside. I glanced up at Nick still in the tiller seat, but he was staring straight up the hill, with parted lips and bright eyes. He looked like he was about to cream in his jeans. I looked up too, and this time I could see the flames, roaring up into the sky. Somebody's mansion along the ridgecrest collapsed in an explosion of flying embers and smoke. The houses on either side of it were blazing like jamboree bonfires. And we were heading right for it.

After a couple of minutes we came abreast of one of the pumper trucks. The houses around us had not caught fire yet, but we could see the flames sweeping down the hillside towards them. Without a word, we dismounted and hooked up a couple of hoses to the truck. We all grabbed them and aimed high, towards the nearest bank of fire. It hissed and sputtered, and fresh smoke poured out into the sky.

Chavez came up to me and grabbed my arm to get my attention. He tugged on Nick's sleeve as well. "I want you two to grab a hose and go up that street," he said, pointing to our left. "Find a hydrant and start dousing the area. The wind is shifting to the west and carrying embers down in that direction. Do what you can to keep any new fires from starting." I started to pull away, but he held on to my arm and tugged me back. "And for God's sake, don't wander off too far from the truck! Any sign of trouble, get your asses back here pronto!" Beneath the soot, his face was grim. Nick and I nodded. We grabbed a hose and scurried off towards the direction Chavez had pointed.

After about a block, we found a hydrant and hooked up to it. Chavez was right about the wind shift. Burning embers started falling down among us, sometimes winking out, occasionally starting small brush fires. We hosed them down whenever one started, but the embers kept coming down at increasing frequency. It looked more and more like a losing proposition.

Nick pointed further down the street. "There's more smoke coming down from there," he said. "I wouldn't be surprised if there was another bank of fire coming our direction." He didn't seem overly concerned about this. "Let's go check it out."

The son of a bitch has a death wish, I thought. "Hell, no," I said. "We're in no way prepared to take on another fire by ourselves. We're heading back to the truck right now!"

Nick didn't say anything, but just kept staring off down the street towards the smoke. I was prepared to strongarm him and drag him back. He pointed ahead and towards the left. "Looks like we're not alone," he said mildly.

I looked towards where he was pointing. And I saw it too. A figure was silhouetted on a housetop, about a block away, hosing down his roof. "Sweet Jesus," I groaned. "We got to get that idiot down from there fast!"

"Let's go, then," Nick said. He started running down the street towards the man on the roof. I followed right after him, cursing.

By the time we got there, the smoke had surrounded us and visibility wasn't more than fifteen or twenty feet. The house was a split level ranch house, one story only, and the man on the roof was just a few feet above us.

"Get down from there!" I shouted up at him. "The fire's going to be here any minute now!"

The man turned and looked down at us, and I saw with a shock that he was just a kid, early twenties, max. He wore the same stunned, disbelieving expression I had seen on the faces of the other refugees fleeing from the flames. "I got to save this place!" he shouted back. "It's my folks' home." A burning ember fell on the roof a few feet away, and he quickly hosed it down.

The flames were visible now behind the smoke. A half a block down an electrical transformer exploded. A little farther away auto alarms started blaring as the cars parked in the street ignited. "Get the fuck down from there!" I screamed at him in my best drill sergeant's voice. That did the trick. The young man scurried across the roof and down a ladder propped up against the wall. "Is there anybody else in this house?" I barked. The young man shook his head. "Then let's go!"

The three of us started running down the street towards the direction where the fire truck was parked. I began to feel the heat on my back, and the smoke swirled around us thicker than ever. There was a muffled roar behind us, like a crowd at a World Series game witnessing a grand slam homerun. I had no idea how much farther we had to go, but it was clear that the fire was gaining. Another electrical transformer exploded, this time directly behind us.

"We're not going to make it back to the truck in time," Nick shouted. He was breathing heavily but his face was still calm. *What does it take to get a rise out of this guy?* I thought.

"You got any ideas?" I shouted back, trying to match his calm. I was suddenly aware that I desperately had to piss.

Nick looked around. There was a brief shift of wind and the smoke thinned slightly. "Over there," he pointed. "Is that a swimming pool?"

I trained my eyes in the direction he pointed. We were looking at a low sprawling home. Part of its backyard was visible, and I could just barely make out what looked like a strip of concrete and a chrome ladder. "Yeah, I think you're right!" I shouted back. I glanced at the kid. His eyes were glassy with terror. "Come on!" I shouted at him. "Follow us!"

The three of us bolted across the front lawn, down the grass strip that flanked the house and into the backyard. Flames were almost goosing us. There, surrounded by a low mesh fence and strip of concrete, a swimming pool stretched out before us like a vision from heaven. We vaulted over the fence and jumped in.

The neighboring house burst into flames and we felt a rush of heat roll over us. Nick looked at me. "I don't know about you but I'm getting out of this damn gear. I feel like I'm roasting." It wasn't a bad idea, and I followed his example, shrugging out of my heavy coat and helmet. I turned to the kid to see how he was doing.

"You all right?" I asked.

He nodded, but didn't say anything. For the first time I really looked at him. My earlier impression was right; he was young all right, maybe still in his late teens. He had a thatch of sandy hair, light blue eyes, and a face that belonged on a Wheaties box. Under the UCLA T-shirt and cut-offs that he was wearing, his body was tight and fit. He wasn't beefy, but his arms, chest and legs had a muscularity about them that made me suspect he was a jock.

I made an attempt at an encouraging smile. "What's your name?" I asked.

Flaming embers were raining down on the house behind us. The roof started smoking. The young man turned and stared at me with unfocused eyes. For a second I thought he wasn't going to answer me. He licked his lips. "Dave," he mumbled.

I squeezed Dave's arm. Even in all this danger I couldn't help noticing the impressive bulge of his bicep. "We'll get out of this okay, Dave," I said. Once again I pasted a smile on my face. If it looked as phony as it felt, I imagined Dave found it anything but reassuring. Dave looked past me. The expression on his face changed to surprise.

I looked behind me. Nick had stripped down to his bikini briefs, and now was in the process of tugging them down.

"What the hell are you doing?" I asked, stunned.

Nick grinned at me and his eyes shone with excitement. His face was fearless, lit with joy. He looked almost deranged. "I'm just getting comfortable," he laughed. He kicked off his briefs and tossed them further down the pool. His dick was half-hard and rapidly growing. Flames were now crackling on the roof of the house behind us, and a trail of fire was making its way down the exterior walls. The houses on either side of us were yellow-orange fire balls. Nick tossed back his head and laughed. "Ain't this a bitch!" he shouted. He threw back his head and gave a long wolf howl. "I am the God of Hellfire!" he sang.

He glanced over at Dave. His face was almost a caricature of shock, his mouth hanging open, his eyes almost wide enough to pop out. "Is this guy really a fireman?" he asked, awed.

All at once the shock, the adrenalin rush, the terror, the *weirdness* hit me like a thunderclap. I threw back my head and laughed. Dave's eyes bulged out even further, something I didn't think possible, and that just made me laugh all the harder. Nick joined in, and then, amazingly, so did Dave. The roof of the house behind us collapsed with a loud roar and we laughed even harder. It was all tinged with hysteria of course, at least for me and Dave, but there was something exhilarating about all this as well. All bets were off, now; there was nothing any further we could do to save ourselves, and I was ready for anything. Nick pulled me over to him and we kissed long and hard, our tongues crammed deep down each other's throat. *What the fuck,* I thought. *This is probably the last time I'm ever going to get off. I might as well go out with a bang.* I wrapped my hand around Nick's dick and began to stroke it. I always loved the way his cock filled my palm, sliding in and out of my curled fingers like it had a mind of its own. Nick pulled his body close to mine and ground his hips against me. He unzipped my fly and pulled down my pants. Liberated, my cock sprang to full attention, slapping hard against my belly. I shrugged off my shirt and stepped out of my pants. Waves of heat played upon my naked skin.

I felt a hand squeeze my ass and I turned around, surprised. Dave stared back at me with wild eyes. He had already whipped out his cock and was beating off with quick short strokes. He stopped for a second, peeled his shirt off, and tossed it over by Nick's fire-engine-red briefs, floating in the deep end of the pool. His body was hairless and tanned, the color of rich mocha, and ripped in a way that spoke of weeks spent working out in the university gym. His hand slid down between the crack in my ass, and I could feel his finger rubbing up against my bunghole. I didn't know if he naturally swung towards guys, but I guess there's something about facing imminent death that will encourage you to take whatever's available. Nick dropped down to his knees in the shallow water and took my dick in his mouth. His lips slid up and down the shaft, and he twisted his head from side to side for maximum sensory effect. Nick always did know how to give terrific blow jobs. He threw himself wholeheartedly into sucking cock, like just about everything else he did.

Dave wrapped his arms around me from behind, sliding his strong hands up and down my torso. He rubbed his thumbs over my nipples, then squeezed them hard. I groaned loudly. I reached behind and cupped his balls in my hand. They had a meatiness and heft to them that gave my dick an extra throb. Dave pressed his body tight against mine, his thick cock sliding up and down my ass crack. I turned my head and we kissed hard, our tongues wrapping around each other. I closed my eyes and let the sensations caused by Nick's mouth and Dave's hands and tongue sweep over me. Fire-heated pool water lapped around my thighs and each breath I took seared my lungs. The flames around us were consuming most of the oxygen and I felt dizzy from the lack of it. It gave the sex a dreamy, unreal quality, nightmarish but exciting at the same time.

Dave's cockhead poked against my bunghole, and I knew he meant to fuck me. "Hold on a second," I said. I reached for my pants, pulled the condom out of my back pocket, and handed it to him. He stared at it stupidly, like I had just given him a rubber chicken.

Nick took my cock out of his mouth and laughed. "I don't believe it!" he said.

"Believe it," I replied.

Nick shook his head and grinned. "You're like the guy in front of the firing squad who won't smoke a last cigarette because it's bad for his health."

"We still might get out of this," I said sharply. I thrust the condom into Dave's hand. "You want to fuck, put it on." Without argument, Dave unrolled the condom down his dick shaft and spit in his hand. He stroked his cock a couple of times for extra hardness and then pushed it between my ass cheeks. I bent over to make it easier for him. With excruciating slowness he worked his dick inch by inch up my ass. I closed my eyes and grimaced from the pain, momentarily forgetting about the fire. I made a vow that if ever I survived this, I would include a tube of lube in my standard fire fighting kit. Dave began pumping his hips, sliding his dick in and out of my chute; the pain subsided and soon was replaced with the exquisite sensation of having my ass full of cockmeat. I began moving my body in sync with Dave's, meeting him thrust for thrust. Dave groaned his appreciation. I felt my dick regain its hardness and I started beating off. Nick made a motion to take it in his mouth again.

"No," I gasped. "Stand up, I want dick in both ends."

Nick straightened up, grinning. His dick thrust out in front of him, thick and implacable, the head flared, demanding to be sucked. The heat of the fire around us had made his balls hang loose and heavy; I rolled them gently in my hand as I slid my mouth down his shaft. Since my first taste of it in the firehouse shower room, Nick's dick has always felt like it was made for my mouth; the fit seemed almost too perfect to be an accident. My tongue played upon it, teased it, working it back into the deeper reaches of my throat.

Nick started pumping his hips, deliberately synchronizing his thrusts with Dave's. *Thrust in* and I was stuffed with dickmeat from both ends, *pull out*, and I was left empty and greedy for more. Nick reached over and squeezed Dave's nipples, never falling out of the rhythm the two of them had set. They were dancing together, using me as a conduit to have sex with each other as well as me. My dick gave an extra throb just thinking about this, and I felt my balls pull up in anticipation of the load I was about to blow.

Dave started moaning, and I felt the grip of his arms around my torso get tighter. "Yeah," Nick grunted. "Shoot that load up his ass." Dave quickened his thrusts and suddenly his body began to shudder. He cried out as I felt the pulse of his dick squirting his cum into the condom up my ass. As if on cue, Nick suddenly pulled his dick out of my mouth and a gush of jizz spewed onto my face, and then another, and another. It dripped down my cheeks and chin, thick and viscous. I wiped my hand across my face and then wrapped my cum-drenched fingers around my dick again. A few quick thrusts into my fist and I was off and running too, squirting cum into the heated pool water as if it were on fire and I was hell bent on putting it out. The flames around us roared and smoke filled our lungs. I could feel the skin on my face begin to blister from the heat. We collapsed into the deeper waters of the pool and waited, exhausted, for whatever was going to happen to go ahead and take its course.

As it turned out, we survived. Through the quirk of a wind shift, the fire marched on to the north and left the yard around the pool unscathed. It was only after the fire around us had subsided to smoldering rubble that we finally risked leaving the safety of the pool. The hot coals on the ground soon burned through Dave's tennies, and Nick and I had to cut pieces of our coats off and wrap them around his feet. But we made it back to safety eventually. The other guys in our team had given us up for dead and were stunned when we finally showed up. To his acute embarrassment, Chavez started bawling like a baby.

The miraculous survival of two firemen and a college kid is the kind of story that the media loves. We made the front page of all the local papers and even a sidebar in *Time*. It was clipped and posted on the firehouse locker room bulletin board, with the words "local heroes make good" scrawled on top.

Nick and I read it together. It was late at night, and we were just turning in from our shift.

I turned to Nick and grinned. "If they only knew the whole story, Christ, would that ever knock their socks off!"

Nick laughed. He glanced into the darkened dorm room. "It looks like everyone's asleep," he said. His mouth curved up into a sly grin.

"Cut it out, Nick," I laughed, shaking my head. "We have to start acting like responsible adults."

But Nick just pulled me towards him and planted his mouth on mine. After a few seconds I reached down and unzipped his fly. "Come on," I growled. "We haven't done it by the water cooler, yet."

SIXTY-NINING ON A STORMY SEA

I'M DREAMING that I'm swinging in a hammock gone amok, pitching wildly back and forth, when a hand roughly shakes my shoulder. I open my eyes and see Jonas' face looming over me, a big, silly grin on it. I know that grin; I also know that gleam in his eyes. "Go away," I mumble, turning over on my side. "I'm trying to sleep."

But Jonas will have none of that. "C'mon, Chris," he croons in my ear. "I've been fighting a storm for four fuckin' hours while you been sawing logs. I need a little loving to get me feeling good again." He slides a hand underneath the blanket and squeezes my cock. His hand is like a block of ice.

"Christ!" I cry out, bolting up. Jonas laughs and I glare at him. But I see by the light of the lantern swinging overhead that he's shivering and that his hair is plastered down against his skull by rain and seawater. I also notice the rings of exhaustion under his eyes. The *Billy B.* (named after an old boyfriend of Jonas', long since sailed off to other ports) is pitching a lot steeper than when I got off my own watch, four hours ago, and the wind is howling like a sonuvabitch. Tiger, the third member of our crew, is going to have his hands full for the next four hours as Jonas' relief.

"Come on," I growl, lifting up the blankets. "Get your things off and climb in."

Jonas doesn't have to be told twice. With a wide grin, he shucks off his clothes and dives under the blankets. He wraps his powerful arms around me and pulls me against him in a tight bear hug. His skin is wet and clammy, but he's shivering less now; we just lie there, quietly, letting the boat rock us as Jonas' body takes on my own heat. Jonas sighs in contentment and then kisses me lightly, his beard tickling my chin. He rests his large, calloused hand on my thigh and slowly strokes my leg. I shift my position, snuggling up closer to him, feeling the hard muscularity of his body, the fur of his chest. Jonas' hand slides up and cups my ass as he begins to dry hump my belly with his hard, thick dick.

He reaches down and wraps his hand around both our dicks, stroking them together with a slow, lazy rhythm. The heat of his dick flows into mine, and I can feel the weight of his balls against my thigh. I start pumping my hips, fucking his fist, sliding my dickmeat against his, as I run my hands over his body. His chest is a redwood trunk in a green, quiet forest, his ass is smooth, sun-warmed rock. For a few seconds I forget that I'm on a 36-foot ketch in a South Pacific storm, bobbing between waves as tall as two-story buildings. I give Jonas a long, wet kiss, pushing my tongue deep down his throat. Jonas gives a muffled groan and rolls on top of me.

We thrash around in the bunk, getting tangled up in the blankets, our bodies rocking back and forth as the *Billy B.* fights the storm. Jonas sits on my chest and drops his balls in my mouth; I roll them around with my tongue as he slaps my face with his dick. As I suck on Jonas' fleshy scrotum, I look up at him, past the long expanse of muscled, tattooed flesh, up into his broad, good-natured face. Jonas isn't what you'd call "classically handsome." In fact, a convincing argument could be made that he's downright homely: a bulbous, red nose, a too-wide mouth, two shrewd, blue eyes, small and pig-like. A white, jagged scar streaks from his left ear down under his jawbone like a bolt of petrified lightning (Jonas says he got it in a knife fight in a Suva City bar; according to Tiger, Jonas really got it from tripping on the gangplank while drunk and smashing his face on the rocks below).

Jonas pivots around and takes a firm grasp of my dick. He bends down and runs his tongue around the head, slobbering on it, getting it all juiced up. All I can see of him now is his ass and the slow, heavy swing of his balls. Nature has compensated for Jonas' face by giving him a truly beautiful ass: firm and smooth, pale and perfectly proportioned. I reach up and reverently part the two fleshy half-moons, and his puckered bunghole winks at me. I bury my face in his crack and bathe it with my tongue. Jonas groans, his voice muffled by a mouthful of my dick. I thrust my hips up, shoving my cock deeper down his throat as I chow down on his pink, ocean-bathed sphincter.

I come up for air and begin tonguing Jonas' dick and balls. Jonas shifts his body so that he's lying beside me now rather than on top, giving me full access to his meaty shaft. I pause for a second and gaze at it, all thick and veined, topped with a dark red, uncut knob, already oozing precum. *Just beautiful*, I think. Jonas contracts his asshole and his dick gives a sharp throb. "Do you like what you see, Chris?" he asks, grinning.

"Yeah, Jonas," I laugh. "You're a goddamn miracle of Nature."

Jonas' grin widens. He twitches his fat red dick again, and I have to admit, my mouth fairly waters at the sight of it. "You can suck it now, lad," he growls.

I run my tongue from the base of Jonas' dick slowly up the thick shaft and then swirl it around the swollen knob. Jonas sighs. I suddenly swoop down and work his shaft down my throat, pressing my nose against his black, crinkly pubes. Jonas cries out from the shiver of unexpected pleasure. He gobbles down on my dick with all the enthusiasm of a shark feeding on chum, and we both settle down into the serious business of cocksucking. Sixty-nine is no mean feat when the both of you are being tossed around on a stormy sea like a sack of crabs. Jonas and I roll with the pitch and yaw of the *Billy B.*, sucking and slurping as best we can, making up with our enthusiasm for our lack of finesse.

Jonas' body starts to quiver, and I can feel the jolt of his orgasm sweep across his body. He throws back his head and bellows as the first squirt of jizz hits the back of my throat. I suck eagerly, moving my head back and forth to heighten the sensation of my lips on his dickshaft. Jonas groans mightily as the next jizz wave slams down my throat, and then a third and a fourth. It feels like I've drunk about a quart of the creamy load before Jonas finally rolls over on his back, panting.

"Shoot on my face, Chris," he growls. "Slime it up good."

I'm only too happy to oblige. I straddle his chest and fuck my fist furiously. The boat makes a wild plunge down a wave trough, and the lamp swings wildly. It's like having sex on a goddamn roller coaster. Jonas reaches up and gives my nipples a sharp twist, his eyes drilling into mine. That's all I need to push me over the edge. I close my eyes and cry out, feeling my dick pulse in my hand as my load spews out and splatters against Jonas' face. When I'm done, his cheek and chin are smeared with the ropy strands of my jizz. I bend down and kiss Jonas tenderly and then lick his face clean. He pulls me down and envelops me in his huge arms, and we lie there, flesh to flesh, as the boat heaves and the winds howl at near-typhoon speeds. Eventually, I drift off into sleep.

It seems like I've just shut my eyes when I hear Tiger bellowing from above deck: *"Get your ass up here, Chris, and relieve me!"* *Oh, shit!* I think. I disentangle myself from Jonas' arms and scramble out of my bunk, hurriedly pulling on my clothes. Jonas mumbles something, turns over on his side, and falls back to sleep. The wind is still howling, and the *Billy B.* is leaping up and down the waves as wildly as ever. I don my foul weather gear and climb up the ladder.

It's 0400 and pitch black. The wind slams into the plexiglass of the cabin, pelting it with sheets of rain. Tiger is at the helm staring grimly ahead, for all the good that'll do. We can't even see the *Billy B.*'s bow, much less what's ahead of us. Our world has shrunk to the red glow of the binnacle. With his salt-and-pepper beard and hard, gray eyes, Tiger looks like an extra out of *Moby Dick*. He swings his gaze towards me and I make a point not to flinch. Tiger was born sailing boats and has been zigzagging across the Pacific for the past thirty-five years. Jonas and he go back a long ways, even though Jonas is a good twenty years younger, so he gives Jonas some slack. But Tiger regards me as the purest greenhorn, a landlubber, a dumb kid, and, at best, treats me with a gruff tolerance. Right now, Tiger's look tells me he's got me classified somewhere around "fishbait."

He steps aside from the helm and I take over the wheel. "It's a son of a bitch out there," he growls. "The winds are up to 50 knots, though they're still blowing from the northeast. It'll take all you got just to keep on course." He gives me a piercing look. "Do you think you're up for it?"

I give an irritated laugh. "Do I have a choice?"

Tiger's look doesn't waver. I can see the doubt in his eyes, and my irritation flares up. "Why don't you get some sleep?" I say, trying to keep the anger out of my voice.

Tiger doesn't say anything for another few seconds. He finally turns and starts climbing down the ladder. "Wake me up if you need any help," he mutters over his shoulder.

The course we're sailing at is 55 degrees east northeast, keeping us running with the storm. There may be some tacking involved, but, according to Tiger and Jonas, we should get to Honolulu within nine days. I think about beaches of fine-grained, white sand, fringed by palms, of land that stays put when you walk on it, the same way a starving man thinks about a T-bone steak. I hold on to the wheel, eye fixed on the compass set in the binnacle. The sails are all down, of course, except for the staysail, and the shrouds scream bloody hell in the rising winds. The blackness outside is so thick I feel that if I reached out and closed my hand, it would ooze between my fingers like mud. Each time the *Billy B.* charges forward into an approaching wave, gallons of water pour into the cockpit; it only takes a couple of minutes for me to be completely soaked. For about the millionth time I wonder what the fuck I was thinking of when I let Jonas talk me into signing aboard this cruise. Right now I could be spending my summer playing volleyball on the Venice beaches and cruising the West Hollywood bars on Santa Monica Boulevard.

As the hours go by, the sky lightens to an iron-grey; by the time I hit the last half hour of my watch, the night has pretty much disappeared. At 0800 Jonas climbs up into the cockpit from below, his eyes still scrunched up from sleep. He wraps his arms around me from behind, and I feel the bulge of his crotch push against me. I've been up here alone battling the elements for the past four hours, and his body feels awfully damn good. Frankly, I'm just glad for some human company. At this point, even Tiger would look good.

I turn my head around, and Jonas and I exchange a long, wet kiss, with plenty of tongue action. His hands slide under my shirt, the callouses scraping against my skin with an agreeable roughness. He grips each of my nipples between his thumbs and forefingers, and gives them a good tweak.

"How you doing?" he murmurs in my ear.

"A lot better, now," I grin. "It's good to see you."

Jonas' hands slide down my jeans and cup my crotch. "You ain't so hard on the eyes yourself, little buddy," he growls.

I laugh. "You know, whenever you call me 'little buddy,' I think of the Skipper and Gilligan."

Jonas gives a sly smile. "That's just who we are, little buddy. The Skipper and Gilligan."

By early afternoon, the storm begins to break up. The rain has stopped and the wind has died down to thirty knots. The seas are still rough, but I don't get this feeling anymore that we're skirting disaster. That is until Tiger comes clomping up the ladder, his face like the Grim Reaper's.

"There's a crack in our fresh water tank," he says gruffly. "Just about all of our drinking supply has leaked out into the bilge."

Jonas has been taking a reading of our position with the sextant. He lowers his arms. "Shit!" is all he manages to say.

Tiger holds up a jerry can. "I was able to fill this before all the water leaked out. I don't think it'll last us til we get to Honolulu, though."

My gaze shifts from face to face. "Is this where one of us volunteers to jump overboard?" I ask.

Jonas gives a thin smile. "Of course, we don't hear about this until after the rain has stopped," he says. He goes back to his sextant as if nothing has happened.

Six days later and we're down to two cups a day per person. The weather has been fair the entire time. Somebody up there has a lousy sense of humor.

I'm the first to see the ship, twenty degrees off the starboard bow. It's late morning, and my watch is just about winding down. I call down the hatch, "Hey, guys, there's someone out here!"

Jonas and Tiger scramble up the ladder. Jonas peers out of the binoculars. "It's some kind of fishing boat," he says. When Tiger hails it on the radio, all he gets is Spanish in return. Jonas takes over, speaking rapidly. He ends transmission, looking up at us and grinning. "It's a Peruvian tuna clipper. They've agreed to give us enough fresh water to get to Honolulu."

The boat changes course and pulls up about thirty feet from us. Jonas and I row across in the *Billy B.*'s inflatable dinghy, with as many empty cans as we can get our hands on. The clipper is pretty weather beaten, its paint job peeling and the upper part of its hull covered in barnacles. I can just make out the name, *Celestina*, in flaking red paint. We scramble aboard. It seems like the boat has just hauled in a load of fish; tuna lie on the deck in silver piles, some still flapping around.

The crew consists of two brothers who introduce themselves as Rodrigo and Jose. Rodrigo seems the elder, mid twenties, maybe, tall, powerfully built, with a three-day stubble and thick, black moustache. His dark eyes regard us shrewdly. Jose is shorter and wirier, with a more open, almost baby face. He seems just barely out of his teens, a year or two younger than me. He flashes us both a smile that gleams in his dark face.

Jonas and I fill our cans, Jonas chattering in Spanish with the two of them. Rodrigo pulls out a grey metal flask and passes it around. I sniff cautiously when it's my turn. Bourbon, pretty rotgut stuff. That doesn't prevent me from taking a deep swig. By the fourth pass-around, things have loosened up quite a bit.

Rodrigo says something to Jonas without taking his eyes off of me. Jose grins, and so does Jonas. He looks at me and winks. "Rodrigo thinks you're very good looking," he says.

"How am I supposed to take that?" I ask, laughing.

Jonas shrugs. "It looks like any way you want."

Rodrigo and I exchange a long look. The man's black eyes gleam with unmistakable invitation. He has a sensual mouth, full and red; his shirt is unbuttoned, affording a glimpse of a smooth, well-muscled torso. I glance over at Jose, and see the same light in his eyes. Suddenly he doesn't look like such a kid anymore.

I turn to Jonas. "Do these guys speak any English?" I ask him.

Jonas shakes his head. "Not as far as I can tell."

"They're a couple of horny bastards," I say. "What do you say, should we go for it?"

Jonas glances at the two brothers, and they grin and nod their heads at him. Apparently their invitation isn't limited just to me. "Hell, yeah!" Jonas laughs. "You have to ask?" He pulls off his T-shirt, and motions for Jose to come over.

Jose is only too happy to oblige. He walks up to Jonas and runs his hands over Jonas' muscular chest. Jonas cups his hand behind the young man's neck and pulls him close. He kisses Jose hard, their mouths working together, their hands exploring each other's bodies. Jonas begins unbuckling Jose's belt.

Rodrigo walks over to me and lightly lays his hand on my chest. He towers over me, a good three or four inches taller, and I look up into his face. He's still smiling, but his eyes are calculating. His forehead is lined with sweat; I can see drops of it sparkle in his thick eyebrows. He bends down and kisses me, thrusting his tongue deep down my throat. I can smell the whiskey on his breath, and his body stinks of sweat and fish. I breathe it all in, my dick springing up hard. I slide his shirt off his shoulders and it drops to the deck. I lift his left arm and burrow my face in his smelly pit.

I glance over in Jonas' direction. He's turned away from me, and I take in his bull-muscled back, the clench and relaxing of his smooth, perfect ass as he plows Jose's mouth. I reach over and run my hand down the curve of his spine, feeling the play of muscles beneath my finger tips. I give his butt a squeeze and then pry his ass crack open with my fingers. Jonas turns his head towards me and gives me a randy grin and a wink. I wink back and then turn back to Rodrigo and kiss him again, shoving my tongue deep into his mouth. I drag my tongue down his neck, across his chest, swirling it around his nipples. Rodrigo bends down his head and croons a low torrent of words in my ear, his voice guttural and thick. My own crash course in Spanish sex talk 101. I bend my knees and drag my tongue down Rodrigo's torso, across the hard ridges of his belly.

I kneel before him, my knees scraping against the fish scales and sea slime that coat the deck. Rodrigo's cock looms above my face, as thick and gnarled as a madrone root. For the past five months I've been feeding exclusively off of Jonas' meat; I know his fat, pink cock and plump balls as well as I know my own. Rodrigo is such a contrast, his dick a rich, dark coffee, the head flared and purple, his balls hanging heavy in a fleshy sac as black and velvety as twilight. I bury my nose in them and breathe in the rank, musky odor; Rodrigo's body is just a garden of ripe stinks. I open my mouth and suck his balls in, washing them with my tongue. Rodrigo slaps my face with his dick, and I feel the smear of his pre-cum against my cheek. I look up, my mouth full of scrotal flesh, across the long expanse of Rodrigo's tightly muscled body. Framed by blue sky, Rodrigo looks down at me and smiles, his teeth flashing white in his dark face, his eyes bright and shrewd.

Rodrigo buries his fingers into my shaggy hair and with a quick snap of his wrist, yanks my head back. The gesture is rough, almost violent, and I feel a flash of anger. But Rodrigo just gives a low laugh. He traces his fingers down my face, across my lids and cheeks, cradling my chin with his hand as his eyes burn into mine. He gently lays his fingers across my lips. I open my mouth and suck them in, licking the fish taste from them. Rodrigo removes his fingers and replaces them with his stiff cock. Grasping my head with both hands, he begins pumping his hips, grinding them against my face as his cock pushes hard against the back of my throat. I close my eyes and sink into the sensation of having a mouthful of new cock to play with. Rodrigo fucks my face with slow, easy strokes, growling to me in Spanish. I twist my head from side to side to give him the full benefit of my lips against his tender shaft. He groans appreciatively and quickens the pace of his thrusts.

I glance over towards Jonas and Jose. Jose is flat on his back on a pile of dead fish, with Jonas sprawled on top of him, dry humping his belly. A few dying tuna flap around them.

Jonas glances towards me. "Damn!" he growls. "This boy is practically begging for a serious fucking, and I don't have any rubbers!"

I reach over and grab my shorts and pull out the mini-pack of condoms. I tear one off and toss it to Jonas. Jonas stares at the foil package in his hand and then at me. "How the hell did you wind up carrying these?" he asks, half in awe.

"I pulled them out of storage this morning, right before my watch," I say. "I was going to replenish the supply under my bunk." I grin. "Isn't that what you're always trying to teach me about sailing? Anticipate all emergencies?"

Jonas just shakes his head as he sheaths his dick. I turn to Rodrigo again. With my eyes never leaving his face, I tear off the top of the foil with my teeth and pull a condom out. Rodrigo's dark eyes watch me intently. I unroll the condom down his dick shaft and then pull him down towards me. Rodrigo doesn't waste any time. He pins me against the deck with a brawny forearm and then hoists my legs over his shoulders. He scoops up a handful of fish slime from a puddle on the deck and liberally slicks his cock with it. I wrap my legs around Rodrigo's torso and relax as he slowly impales my ass. Rodrigo's eyebrows are pulled down in concentration, and a low grunt escapes his mouth as he slides inside me. For a couple of heartbeats, we lie motionless together, almost breathless, as my asshole says hello to Rodrigo's cock. Then, with a gentleness that surprises me, he slowly pumps his hips. I push up to meet him, and he picks up the pace, slamming into me hard enough to make his balls slap against me.

It's late afternoon, and the sun beats down on us, its heat reflecting off the slick deck. Sweat trickles down Rodrigo's face and splashes on to mine. I reach up and twist his nipples, not gently. He bares his teeth in a fierce smile and grinds his hips hard against me; it feels like I have about two feet of cock in me. I squeeze my ass muscles hard, clamping down on Rodrigo's cock. He gasps and then gives off a long, trailing groan. I arch my back up and squeeze again. Rodrigo groans again, louder, his eyes wide and startled. *That's right,* I think. *I know a few tricks that can make this a ride you won't soon forget.* I push my hips up to meet Rodrigo, matching the rhythm of his thrusts, and start beating off, timing my strokes to the pounding Rodrigo is giving my ass.

The stench of fish is overwhelming; it defines everything else, addles my sun-baked brain. This whole experience takes on a hallucinatory buzz. Fucking is fish, and I am the goddamn catch of the day, skewered by the dick of the cosmic Fisherman. Things fall apart into a chaos of images: Rodrigo's black, snapping eyes, his sweat-drenched torso, the boat's mast pitching and yawing above us, the creak of the rigging, the blazing, tropical sun, Jonas' loud grunts, the flapping bodies of dying tuna all around us . . .

Rodrigo has quickened his pace; his dick slams into my ass with a punishing regularity, and little whimpers escape from his open mouth. I reach down and give his balls a good squeeze, and Rodrigo throws back his head and groans loudly. His body trembles violently and I feel his load pulse out of his dick and squirt hard into the condom up my ass. A few, quick strokes of my hand pushes me over the edge as well. My dick gives a sharp throb and the orgasm sweeps over me, my jizz squirting out onto my belly, my chest, my face. I cry out as my spunk gushes, and Rodrigo growls his approval. He collapses on top of me, pushing his tongue into my mouth. We kiss feverishly as the last of the sex spasms pulse through our bodies.

I glance over towards Jonas and Jose and get an eyeful of Jonas' ass pumping away, his balls swinging like a ship's bells on heavy seas. Their bed of fish is now pretty much scattered, and tuna bodies lie strewn all over the deck. Jonas has wrapped his powerful arms around Jose in a bear hug and is giving that boy the ride of his life. Jose groans, and Jonas joins in, his moans rising in pitch and volume. Suddenly he pulls out, rips the condom off, and starts jacking off. His body shakes violently, and a thick, ropy wad of jizz squirts out of his dick onto Jose's face. This is followed by another spurt, and then another. Jose opens his mouth to receive the spermy rain, lapping it up hungrily. He groans, and I see his own load ooze out between his fingers. Jonas shakes his body like some old mutt caught in the rain; drops of sweat scatter off him. He looks at me with eyes glassy from heat and spent sex, but the silly-ass, lopsided grin on his face is the same as ever.

"Damn, Chris," he laughs. "That was sure a kick in the ass!"

I laugh, but don't say anything.

We row back to the *Billy B.* with our water containers full. Tiger eyes us suspiciously as we scramble aboard but says nothing. I know he's curious about why we took so long, but he'll be damned if he's going to break down and ask us. Jonas hands over a couple of the containers for Tiger to stow.

Tiger wrinkles his nose. "Christ!" he exclaims. "You stink worse than a beached whale."

"Well, hell, Tiger," Jonas says, all innocence. "We were on a tuna boat. What do you expect?"

Jonas and I later dive naked into the ocean to try to clean off the stink (though I have a feeling we'll be smelling of fish for days after we reach port in Honolulu). The Pacific is as warm as bathwater and stretches out around us like a sheet of polished metal. The *Celestina* is now just a dot on the western horizon, and Rodrigo and Jose have been reduced to a hot memory. Jonas is more playful than ever. He grabs my legs from below and gives me a good dunking before swimming back to the *Billy B.* I tread water, watching him climb aboard, taking in his beautifully muscled body. That little adventure on the *Celestina* has just whetted my appetite for more; my dick is already hard thinking about the things I'm going to do to Jonas. I swim back to the *Billy B.*, cutting through the water with long, easy strokes, knowing that Jonas is stretched out naked on the deck waiting for me.

PAGAN DICKMEAT

I'M THIGH DEEP in warm, still water, the sun pouring down on my head and shoulders, and the only thought going through my mind right now is which one of the Valjean brothers looks better naked. I'm willing to give a lot of thought to this question. It's hard to imagine that Pierre and Claude are even *related*, much less brothers. Pierre is a strapping good-natured ox of a man, well over six feet tall, with broad shoulders and a powerful chest and arms. He's typical of the Normandy French: blonde, smooth, fair-skinned, with eyes that are a startling blue. Claude, on the other hand, is pure Mediterranean: lithe, compact, dark, with crisp black hair and black eyes that sparkle with intelligence and humor. Pierre towers over him, and right now I watch as he picks his younger brother up and laughingly tosses him a good eight feet into the deeper water. Claude swims back with quick, powerful strokes, dives beneath the surface and topples Pierre. They wrestle playfully for a few minutes, and this distraction allows me to take in their naked bodies without fear of being noticed. The French appreciate subtlety.

Yeah, they don't have anything in common except one thing: they both have dicks of death: fleshy, meaty schlongs that just beg to be sucked. Though even there there are differences: Pierre's dick is a faint pink, laced with blue veins snaking along its trunk. A dark red head peaks out through the wrinkled foreskin. Claude's cock, however, is a rich mocha that blossoms into a dark brown mushroom head. While Pierre's dick, though formidable, is in proportion to the rest of his massive body, Claude's is startling: swinging from that wiry, compact body it commands attention of the most mouth-watering kind.

I hear a woman's voice calling and see Marie, Pierre's wife on the bank, their young boy, Jacques, pressed against her thigh, sucking his thumb. Therese, Claude's girlfriend stands next to her and waves. My first instinct is to sink into the water and hide my half hard dick out of a rush of unexpected modesty. But the ladies seem to take our nudity matter-of-factly, and so I remain standing, smiling politely, feeling slightly ridiculous.

"We just came to tell you that the picnic is all spread out," Therese calls. "If you don't come in now, we'll eat it all ourselves!"

We wade ashore and pull on our clothes. I manage to sneak a last glance at the Valjean brothers' meaty cocks before they pull their trousers up. I hope their women appreciate what they have. A brief picture flashes through my mind of Pierre pumping my ass vigorously as sexy Claude fucks my face. I brush the image aside impatiently. I didn't come to France to entertain impossible fantasies.

The spread Marie and Therese have provided is simple but elegant in a way only the French know how: a couple of different patés, several loaves of fresh, still-warm bread, marinated chicken, a boysenberry tart and a quality Bordeau. Like everything else I've seen them do, Claude and Pierre dive into eating with true gusto, burying their faces into the chicken and bread and drinking copious amounts of wine. Therese whispers something into Claude's ear and he throws back his head and laughs in an easy, natural way that is completely charming. Though ignorant of the joke, Pierre grins affectionately at his brother. Even though I've only known them for two days, I'm already half in love with these guys. Claude's eyes meet mine.

"Therese cannot believe how young you are," Claude says, smiling. "When she heard we were to lead another American anthropologist around, she thought it would be someone much, much older." His smile grows sly. "And uglier. Therese thinks you are very handsome. And that your American accent is sexy."

My eyes meet Therese's and I smile. "Actually, I'm not really an anthropologist," I say. "I'm just a graduate student doing research for my thesis. I guess I didn't make myself very clear in my letter."

"Yes, your letter was a little vague," Pierre agrees. He pulls a piece of meat from a chicken bone and pops it into his mouth. "You said you wanted to see the cave paintings in the area, but you didn't say what you were looking for in particular." He pauses and his eyes increase their focus by the barest fraction. "That is if you *are* looking for anything in particular." He leaves the unspoken question hanging in the air. "I'm really not trying to be mysterious," I say, grinning. "I'll be glad to tell you what I'm looking for. The Horned God."

Claude and Pierre exchange glances. Suddenly neither one of them is smiling. "Please explain, Robert," Claude asks quietly.

I'm a little taken aback by their sudden seriousness. "The Horned God," I say. "It's a powerful mythic figure, going back thousands of years. He plays a prominent part in ancient religions throughout the world: Pan, the Minotaur, the Lord of the Underworld. When the Christians came along and started converting the pagans, they didn't know what to do with him. So they made him into the devil. But before that he was always worshipped as something sacred."

Therese leans over and whispers something in Claude's ear, giggling. Claude waves her off. "What does this Horned God mean to you, Robert?" Claude asks. There's a directness to his gaze that I'm beginning to find disconcerting.

"Most of what's written about the cave paintings in France revolves around the Goddess cult, the Great Mother," I reply. "Statuettes have been found of her, paintings, old evidences of sacrifices. It's assumed she was the major deity here. However, I've read a few scattered references about images of a man with antlers and goat feet, sometimes alone, sometimes running through herds of bison or antelope. The Horned God. I want to learn more about him. It's my theory there was a whole counter-cult centered around him, maybe in opposition to the Goddess cult." My eyes flick from Pierre's face to Claude's. "You guys know anything about this?"

Pierre shrugs good-naturedly. "Maybe. Maybe not." He reaches over and refills my cup. "Have some more wine, Robert. This really is a very nice Bordeau."

I take a long sip. The sun beats down on me, hotter than I would have suspected for early June. Pierre grins at me but his eyes are thoughtful. Claude plucks a blade of grass and absently chews on it, his eyes staring off into the distance.

Two weeks have gone by since that picnic, and I'm feeling pissed. I pitch my suitcase on the bed and sling my clothes in haphazardly. My plane leaves tomorrow morning, and the only thing I can think of is what a bust this trip has been. I pick up a shoe and fight the impulse to smash it against the wall.

I hear a knock and Claude comes in. I grunt a greeting and continue packing. Claude leans against the bureau with arms crossed and watches me. "You don't look very happy," he says.

"Why should I be?" I growl. Then I realize how ungracious that sounds. "I'm sorry," I say. "I'm just disappointed about how my trip turned out."

Claude smiles, but his eyes are sympathetic. "Pierre and I took you to dozens of caves," he says. I shrug but don't reply. "You're upset because we didn't show you any paintings of the Horned God, right?"

I throw my shirts in the bag, without looking up. "You got it," I say shortly. As much as I like Claude, I fight the impulse to snap at him. Some guide, I think bitterly.

There's another long silence. Claude clears his throat. "Do you know what today is?"

I push down the lid to my suitcase and click the clasps together. "Yeah, June 20. So what?"

"It's the solstice. The longest day of the year." Claude's expression is mocking. "An important pagan holiday. If you're going to be a student of old religions, Robert, you should know things like that."

I turn and look at him. "So what's your point, Claude?" I don't snarl, but I come damn close. It's his grin that bugs me the most, like he's *amused* by my frustration.

"My point," Claude laughs, "is that I'm willing to take you to see the Horned God now." He arches his eyebrows. "That is, if you're still interested."

I stare at him. "Is this a joke?" I finally ask. Claude's still laughing. He holds his hand out to me. "Come on," he says. "Let's go."

We're in the middle of some field, Claude leading the way with a flashlight, a coil of rope slung over his left shoulder. He stops abruptly, brushing some bushes aside. "Here we are," he says, shining his light on the ground.

I look down. There's an opening into the ground, a hole a couple of feet wide. Claude starts tying the rope around a nearby tree trunk. I peer down the hole and see nothing but blackness. "What's down there," I ask uneasily.

Claude is tying the other end of the rope around his waist. "It's the entrance to a cavern that's about forty feet deep. Pierre and I discovered it years ago when we were kids playing in the field. We're going down into it."

I clear my throat. "Look, why don't we just wait until daylight?"

"Robert," Claude says gently. "It's going to be just as dark down there at daytime as it is at night."

I feel myself blushing at that one, and now I'm grateful it's dark. A thought crosses my mind. "Where's Pierre?" I ask.

Claude starts playing the rope out. He's standing at the lip of the hole, easing himself over the edge. He looks up at me. "Don't worry about Pierre." He pauses. "Robert, you wanted to see the Horned God. I'm going to show him to you. But on one condition. You can't be an anthropologist tonight. You have to be prepared to participate fully in whatever happens. Otherwise, the deal's off." His eyes lock with mine. "Do you agree?" I pause and then nod yes. Claude smiles broadly. "Good. When I get to the bottom, I'll untie the rope. Then you lower yourself down after me." Before I can respond, his head disappears into the hole.

It isn't long before I find myself rappelling down the cave wall in total darkness. *What the hell have I gotten myself into?* I wonder. Claude's flashlight beam finds me from below and guides me down. The air is dank and stale and the blackness is almost suffocating. Claude's face floats before me in the flashlight beam like some apparition. I hear a throbbing which I first think is the blood beating in my ears. After a few seconds I realize what I'm hearing is the faint beat of drums.

Claude smiles. I can see he's very excited. "Follow me," he says, shining the light on the ground. I stumble after him.

After a few minutes I can see a faint light up ahead, firelight, I guess, by its redness and the way it flickers. The drumming is much louder, a steady, pulsing beat, and now I can hear voices chanting along with it. We turn a corner around a rock outcropping, and I stop dead in my tracks.

About eight or nine naked men dance around a large bonfire burning in the middle of a vast rock chamber. One of them beats an elk-hide drum. It takes me a couple of seconds to realize that I know most of these guys: I recognize Louis, the humpy young dairy farmer down the road from Claude and Pierre, and Paul, the village pharmacist's son, and others from the village or neighboring farms. All of the men are young, none over thirty. I scan them all but see no sign of Pierre.

Louis separates from the crowd and walks over to us; his tight, muscled body gleams in the firelight, and there's a sheen of sweat on his face and torso. He also has a roaring hard-on, and makes no effort to conceal it. With more than a little interest, I watch his dick and balls swing from side to side as he gets nearer. He grins and lifts his hand in greeting but says nothing. Claude begins shucking his clothes, and after a brief pause, remembering my promise, I do the same.

In a minute we're as naked as everyone else. Louis is carrying a bowl in his left hand. He offers it to Claude who drinks deeply and then hands it to me. I hesitantly take a sip. The liquid inside is bitter and I almost gag. I force myself to drink the rest and then hand the empty cup back to Louis, grimacing. Louis laughs. There's a wolfish glare in his eyes that I find unsettling as hell. And extremely sexy.

Someone throws a couple of logs onto the fire, and the flames leap up. The sudden flare of light illuminates the far cavern wall for the first time, showing a picture painted on it. I stare in amazement. It's of a man, maybe, but with antlers, goat feet and a horse's tail. Between his legs swings a big bull dick and balls. He's grinning, with wild, mad eyes fixed on us, and he towers over us, at least twenty feet high. The Horned God! I feel a thrill of excitement. This could be the archeological find of the century. I turn to ask Claude about it, but he's off with the other men, dancing.

The drums beat faster now, and the chanting gets louder, wilder. The men dance around the fire, swaying their hips, their movements unambiguously sexual. Most of them have hard-ons now, and as they dance, they run their hands over their bodies, flicking their nipples, pumping their dicks in time to the drums. Claude joins in, laughing, stroking his dick as he circles the flames. His hard-on is thick and impressive. He stares at me in open invitation and I eagerly join the circle. Claude grins and embraces me, his stiff dick dry humping my belly. Whatever it was I drank has started to affect me now; the room seems to spin and my mind reels. Claude works his tongue into my mouth as his hands cup my ass and squeeze. I wrap my hand around his dick and stroke it slowly. The drumming fills my ears, moves through my body, overwhelms my mind. And suddenly stops.

The men quit dancing, and Claude pulls away from me. One man picks up the drum again and begins a slow, reverberating beat. They all turn their heads and peer off into a dark corner of the cave, beyond the range of the firelight. I see movement and a figure slowly emerges from the blackness and approaches us: a tall man with a powerful build, equally nude except for a pair of antlers jutting up from his head. His massive dick thrusts straight out, the swollen head pulled free from the foreskin. I recognize the dick before anything else. It's Pierre.

The men murmur and drop to their knees. I follow suit. They begin a low guttural chant, the words in some language I've never heard, certainly not French or English. Pierre breaks through the ring and stands between us and the fire. His eyes are vacant, his face wears the expression of someone deep in trance. His muscular body is silhouetted, framed by the flames. He slowly approaches the nearest man, who happens to be Louis, and stands before him. Louis looks up at him, an expression of awe on his face. He reaches over and reverently wraps his hand around Pierre's thick cock. Except for the crackling fire, the cavern is completely silent. Louis leans forward and swallows Pierre's dick, inch by inch, until his nose is buried in blonde pubes. His head bobs back and forth as he begins sucking on the giant cock. The other men murmur their approval.

My vision blurs and I strain to focus my eyes again. Whatever Louis gave me to drink must have been some kind of hallucinogen. Everything is taking on an unreal, dreamlike quality. I watch as Pierre moves on to the next man, and then the man after him. Each time the ritual is repeated, each man gets a chance to feed off the Horned God's dickmeat. I'm last in line with Claude kneeling beside me.

Pierre approaches his brother, who is swaying slightly, his eyes half closed. As Pierre towers over him, Claude's eyes widen and his mouth curves up into a blissful smile. He reaches up and runs his hands tenderly over his brother's torso, kneading the hard pectorals, tracing the ridged bands of Pierre's abdominals. Claude leans forward and takes his brother's balls in his mouth, tonguing them gently. His tongue slowly moves up Pierre's hard cock shaft, leaving a wet trail behind. As the other men did before him, he swallows the engorged cock completely. Pierre groans and I'm close enough to see the fever in his eyes. He reaches down with both hands, grasps Claude's head, and begins pumping his hips, fucking his brother's face with long, slow strokes. Claude swallows the meaty dick as best he can, but he does it clumsily, never quite matching the rhythm of Pierre's pumping hips. It's easy to see he hasn't had much experience as a cocksucker. In spite of that, Pierre groans again, the sound trailing off to a loud sigh. He pulls away from his brother, gasping. I wait, with pounding heart, as he turns and approaches me, the last man to receive this communion of sacred dickmeat.

Whatever was in that drink is peaking now. I stare at the blonde naked giant in front of me, wearing stag horns, bathed in firelight, and I feel the rapture and magic too. This is not Pierre who stands before me, his giant cock thrust in my face. Or rather, it's Pierre, but something else as well, something moving *through* Pierre, something that fills the cavern and is timeless. The Horned God.

I hesitantly reach up and grasp the thick cock in front of me. Its heat warms my hand, and I can feel the blood beating in it, pushed down pulse by pulse by Pierre's strong young heart. I have never been so sexually excited in my life. I stare at the cock, at the veins running along the shaft, at the red, blood-engorged head, and like the men before me I take it in my mouth and feel it slide all the way down my throat.

Unlike Claude, though, cocksucking is something I'm a master at. As my lips slide down Pierre's thick shaft, I twist my head from side to side, and let my tongue go wild. The cock meat eases down my throat like butter on a hot skillet, and when I get to the end of it, I pause for a few seconds, savoring the feeling of a mouth crammed with dick. I slowly pull back, washing the thick meat with my tongue all the way up to the cockhead, sucking hard all the time. When my mouth gets back to the cockhead I begin all over again, starting a rhythm accented by long, wet strokes. Pierre's body trembles. I tug on his balls, not gently, feeling the loose folds of scrotum flesh fill my hand. My other hand works its way between his ass cheeks, and I worm a finger up his bunghole. Startled, Pierre involuntarily clamps his ass muscles, and my digit feels encased in a vise of warm velvet. Undeterred, I keep on pushing until I touch the prostate. I wiggle my finger and Pierre lets out a mighty groan. His ass relaxes into surrender, and I begin finger fucking him in earnest now.

I look up at him and our eyes meet. His eyes gleam in the firelight, and his body jerks with each upward thrust of my finger. Sweat trickles down his smooth torso. Pierre bends his knees slightly, inviting me to work my finger higher up his ass. I comply. I begin sucking on his balls, first the left one, then the right, as I stroke his spit-slicked dick with my other hand. I put the entire meaty scrotal sac in my mouth and suck mightily, increasing the speed of my strokes. Out of the corner of my eyes I can see the other men watching us, murmuring, stroking their own dicks as they take in this little show Pierre and I are giving them. Behind and above Pierre, the painted image of the Horned God stares down at me with wild, round eyes.

I bury my face in Pierre's balls and inhale deeply. The musty smell of scrotum fills my nose, intoxicates me. I run my tongue down the dark sweaty path to Pierre's asshole and then back to his balls again. Once more I take them in my mouth and bathe them with my tongue as I stroke his meat. Pierre's body is trembling violently now. I look up at him and our eyes lock. His face is drenched in sweat and his teeth are bared in a soundless snarl. His eyes are frantic. I push my finger hard up his ass again and press his prostate.

That does the trick. Pierre arches his back, throws back his head and bellows. A gusher of jizz squirts out of his dick and splatters hard against my face. Another joins it, and then another. His body is wracked in spasms. He throws his arms out and roars again. The other men join him, yelling at the top of their lungs. I turn and watch as one by one, they spew their loads into the fire. Claude, however, turns towards me as he shoots and I get another gush of jizz splashed against my face. I feel the brothers' loads trickle down my cheeks and into my mouth, and I lick my lips, tasting that sweet jizz. I wipe my hand across my face and then beat off rapidly, fucking my cum-smeared hand with quick, short thrusts. It's only a matter of seconds before I splatter my load into the fire as well.

Pierre sinks to his knees and collapses onto the cave floor. One of his antlers snaps off with a loud crack, but no one seems to mind, the ritual is over now. Claude sits next to him and puts his arm around Pierre's shoulder. The gesture is purely brotherly. Pierre opens his eyes and smiles, and this time it's the easy, friendly grin of the old Pierre. There's a drop of cum hanging from the head of his softening dick, and it's all I can do to keep from bending over and licking it off.

Our eyes meet. "This goes on every equinox and solstice, huh?" I ask. "The Celebration of the Horned God?"

Pierre nods but says nothing. He may not be the Horned God anymore, but he's still beautiful. As is Claude, who watches me too, smiling. "You're one of us, now, Robert," he says. "You've gone through the ritual."

I smile too. Already I'm planning my next return. Christmas break should do it. Or rather, the Winter Solstice. One of the men throws another log on the fire and the flames leap up again. The Horned God on the cave wall stares down at us all with his wild eyes.

TRAPPER MEAT

"Six pelts," I said, disgustedly, shaking my head. "I spend a week up at Greenwater Creek trapping beaver, and that's all I get. Six goddamn pelts. Hardly worth the effort. Hell, I remember just five or six years ago I could pull down forty, maybe fifty skins from that creek. It almost ain't worth my while to head out for the trading rendezvous tomorrow with the pitiful load of furs I got this season."

Coyote Jim grunted but didn't say anything. I stared down at the top of his head. Off in the distance a wolf howled so mournful you'd think his heart was breaking. I took a slug of whiskey, swished it around in my mouth and let the liquid fire slide down my throat. "You know," I added, my voice rising, "on my way back I ran into a hunting party of Crees. I recognized one of them from our stay at Fort Defiance last winter. He told me he spotted a feller trapping around by Greenwater, hair the color of a new-polished copper kettle. That was just how he put it. I'll bet you that was McKenzie, snooping around, trapping in the spots *I* staked out years ago. That red-headed sonuvabitch."

Coyote Jim took my cock out of his mouth and glared at me. "Look," he growled. "Do you have to talk about trapping right now? It's ruining the mood."

I looked down at him, taken aback. I suddenly realized I'd not been minding my manners. Here Coyote was knocking himself out to make me feel at home and I was just rattling on about beaver pelts and McKenzie. I gave an embarrassed cough and spat into the fire. "All right, Coyote," I said, "then why the hell don't we just get down to business."

"That's what I been *tryin'* to do," Coyote muttered. But his dark eyes gleamed and I could see the hint of a grin playing around the corners of his mouth. Coyote Jim came close to being about the goddamnedest handsomest man I've ever had the pleasure to come across, white or Injun. His ma was Blackfoot, and he had the high cheekbones, hawk nose and piercing black eyes common to that tribe. But his pa was a white trader, and Coyote had the same tall, big-framed build his old man must have had. Where he got that big, thick dick, though, was anybody's guess. I've seen my share of peckers, both Injun and white, but Coyote's had to take the cake. Except for the red bandanna Coyote always wore around his throat, he was buck naked, and even though his dick was only half-hard now, it already looked bigger than any man could handle. But I always did like a challenge.

I leaned back on my elbows and watched as Coyote's mouth nibbled its way down the length of my dick (a long nibble, I might add). I didn't know whether it's part of some secret Blackfoot teaching, or if Coyote was just a natural, but the man was one powerfully mean cocksucker. He worked my dick with the same easy skill that he rode a horse or skinned an animal. Some folks are just naturally competent, and you just gotta sit back and admire their handiwork when you get to experience it.

I slid down off of the rock I was sitting on and pivoted around so that my head was facing Coyote's bull dick. It lay there stiffening against his thigh, dark and fleshy, like some thick one-eyed snake rearing up, getting ready to strike. I wrapped my hand around it and squeezed. A clear drop of pre-jizz oozed out of the piss slit, and I lapped it up. I pulled back the foreskin, swirled my tongue around the dark knob of his dick, and then slid my mouth down the shaft. Coyote gasped, and he thrust his hips up to meet me halfway. I felt the meaty shaft ram against the back of my mouth and I quickly adjusted my head so that the entire length could slide down my throat. It took a little accommodating, but after a while my nose was buried deep in Coyote's balls. I gave a mighty sniff, savoring that rich, musky smell. Coyote suddenly began fucking my mouth like there was hell to pay. I paid him back in kind, pumping my dick in and out of his mouth with a high-hearted enthusiasm that made my blood sing.

We lay there on the dirt by the campfire, feeding off each other's dicks like it was deep winter and we'd had nothing to eat for weeks. I came up briefly for air. Outside the small circle of light from the fire, the night pressed down upon us like black mud. There was no moon out tonight, and the stars blazed. I looked up the length of Coyote's beautifully muscled body and into his face. In the red glow of the fire he looked more than human, like one of the heroes in the Blackfoot legends he liked to tell me about from time to time.

The tin we kept the cooking grease in was just a few inches away. Coyote reached over, caked his hand with grease and smeared it into the crack of my ass. His finger brushed lightly against my bunghole, teasing it, and then pushed on in. As lubed as it was, it easily slid up my chute to the third knuckle. Coyote began working it in and out, staring into my eyes, his own eyes dark and unreadable, his mouth slightly open. "Your finger feels just fine," I growled, "but I bet your dick would feel a helluva lot better."

"I was thinking the same thing," Coyote grunted. He pivoted around, grabbed my ankles, and slung my legs over his shoulders. Coyote always did tend to get right to the point. His cockhead pushed against my asshole, and I made myself breathe deep and relax, opening up to Coyote as best I could. Coyote slid on in like it was just about the most natural thing in the world. He started pumping his hips, and I just dropped my head down and groaned with pleasure, thinking about all that dick inside of me. I got a dollop of cooking grease myself and started fucking my fist, matching the tempo of Coyote's long, slow strokes. Every now and then he would just keep his dick full up my chute and grind his hips against me. Whenever he did, the night sky would just unfold above me like eagles' wings, beating hard and urgent against my face. I'd cry out and Coyote would laugh at how easily he could overpower me with pleasure. I think he sees that as a weakness in me, but I don't fuckin' care.

Well, Coyote just kept on pumpin' me, working me over like a mountain lion he was trying to bring down. I wrassled him good, snarlin' and spittin', rolling around in the dust by the fire with him, trying to get the best of him. Anybody walking into the campsite would have figured we was fighting each other to the death. Finally I wound up on top. Coyote lay on his back, with something between a grin and a snarl on his face, still driving his dick hard up my ass. His hands slid over my torso, grabbed my nipples and tugged hard on them. That did it for me. I fucked my fist with one last thrust, raised my head to the sky, and howled as my jizz squirted out and splattered hard against Coyote's face. Off in the distance, a couple of wolves howled back. I squeezed my ass tight and clamped down hard on Coyote's dick. He groaned and his whole body shuddered under me as I felt his load squirt up into my ass. I bent down and planted my mouth over his, shoving my tongue deep down his throat.

I could feel his dick soften inside me, but Coyote didn't pull out. I nestled down next to him beside the fire, and he reached over and pulled the buffalo skin over both of us. We fell asleep like that, his arms wrapped around me, his dick still up my ass. That's become our favorite way of sleeping together. A couple of hours later I woke up to the call of a screech owl. Coyote was snoring gently, but his dick was still inside me, half-hard. I nestled closer against him, and just that small movement stiffened his dick to a full boner. Coyote murmured something but never woke up. After a few seconds I drifted off myself.

I woke up for good just before sunrise, when the eastern sky was just turning gray. I kicked the coals to get a fire started again, and boiled water for coffee. By the time Coyote got up, I had a cup waiting for him.

"We got three days hard riding ahead of us before we reach the rendezvous," I said. "Better get your sorry carcass up."

Coyote just yawned and scratched himself. "Hell, Cyrus, if I thought I could trust you to get a good price for my furs, I'd just as soon sit this one out. I just ain't the sociable type." He grinned. "But then, someone's got to keep your ass out of trouble."

I didn't say nothing, but I was glad for Coyote's company. I knew we'd have some high times down there at the rendezvous. And nobody could protect a buddy's back better than Coyote if things took an ugly turn. The sun peeked up over the nearest hill, red as a copper kettle, red as McKenzie's hair. Maybe I'd get a chance to settle some old scores, too, I thought.

By the third night of the rendezvous, I had already just about pissed away all the money the traders had given me for my pelts. Coyote had seen to it on the first day that we'd buy all the provisions we needed for winter before we did anything else. After that and two nights of whiskey drinking and gambling, I was having a hard time finding two coins to rub together. It was getting on in the night, and the campfires were blazing high now. Off in the distance, by the bend in the Sweetwater River, I could see the campfires of the Crows, the Blackfeet, the Bannocks, all the In-juns who had come along to trade too. But around nearby was just the white fur trappers.

I took another hit of whiskey and passed the jug on to Coyote. I could hear the sound of men's voices and laughter from the nearby fire circles. There were shouts coming from one of the more distant fires, and I knew the men were gambling again, tossing bones and betting on which side would land face up. Damn if one of the St. Louis traders hadn't brought a concertina with him, and I heard the music float out over the night. Coyote passed the jug back to me and I drank deep, feeling the whiskey's warmth pass through me and make my body tingle. *This is what a man's life is all about,* I thought. *It don't get no better than this.*

I climbed to my feet again. "I'm going gambling. I still have a couple of bucks left to blow." I looked down at Coyote. "You coming?"

Coyote shook his head. "Naw, I'll just hang out here by the fire." He seemed relaxed again, but he gave me a long, measured look. "You going to stay out of trouble, Cyrus?"

I shrugged and grinned. "I ain't going to go looking for it, Coy-ote. But if trouble comes knocking at my door, I ain't going to hide under the bed neither." I turned and headed towards the fire cir-cle where all the gaming was going on.

I'd been gambling for an hour before McKenzie showed up and joined the circle. I'd seen him around the rendezvous site the past couple of days; hell, with that bright red hair he was easy enough to spot. His eyes were always on me too; I knew he was thinking up some new devilment. But this was the first time we actually got nose to nose. It was a warm summer night, and he was just wear-ing a buckskin vest. The fire light played on his upper body, light-ing up the cut of his muscles, the dusting of red hair across a chest as ripped and powerful as a young buffalo bull's. When he reached up and stretched I couldn't help but notice how his muscles rip-pled, how his biceps bunched together like there was small animals scurrying about under his skin. I'd been winning, and was now up about a hundred dollars and feeling flush. McKenzie looked me in the eye and that wide mouth of his curled up into a slow, friendly grin. With McKenzie, this only meant trouble. He started right up betting against me, and damn if my luck didn't turn sour right away. Hell, I couldn't do nothing right; them bones just kept on turning up wrong, no matter which way I threw them. I knew somehow this was McKenzie's doing. Every time I threw the bones and lost another few dollars to McKenzie, I felt that old heat in me just rise higher and higher. He sat across the patch of dirt, his blue eyes trained on me and I could see the laughter in them, like his gut was just about ready to bust from the joke of it all. I don't think I ever hated that bastard more.

After about a steady hour of losing, I threw the bones to the man next to me. "Well, I'm just about all cleaned out," I grunted. "You take them. I gotta piss." I climbed up unsteadily to my feet and stumbled out into the darkness. I pulled down my buckskin breeches, aimed my dick towards the bushes and let the stream go.

I heard footsteps on dry leaves, and McKenzie came up from behind. "Looks like a good idea," he said. "Mind if I join you?"

I turned to him and scowled. "Yeah, I do. I'm right particular about the company I piss with."

McKenzie grinned. "Too bad." He whipped out his dick and soon there were two streams pouring down the leaves of the bush. McKenzie gave a short laugh. "With all the whiskey I been drinking, I imagine my piss is at least 90 proof. Hell, I should just bottle it. It's a shame to let it go to waste."

"Yeah," I grunted. "You should. You look like a piss drinker."

McKenzie's smile didn't waver a bit, but the light in his eyes turned dangerous. "If I didn't know better, Cyrus," he said calmly, "I'd think that you was trying to insult me." His stream had trickled down to a few drops, and he gave his dick a couple of shakes. But he made no effort to slip his breeches back up. "Well, McKenzie," I drawled, "I guess you *don't* know better. 'Cause that's exactly what I'm trying to do. I know you been nosing around my trapping sites, taking my game. We got some old scores to settle."

"You'd be a hell of a lot more convincing, Cyrus," McKenzie said gently, "if you looked me in the eyes when you said that instead of at my dick."

I jerked my eyes up angrily and glared at him full in the face. "You wave it around, I can't help but look at it," I snapped. But in spite of my best efforts, my eyes shifted down again. His hand was stroking his meat in a slow, teasing manner, and it swelled in his palm, fat and spongy, the head poking out of the foreskin like a prairie dog checking out the weather.

"Come on, Cyrus," McKenzie crooned. "Take a break from that hot half-breed buck of yours. Give someone else a tumble for a change."

I didn't say nothin'. I just stood there, staring at McKenzie's stiff dick, lit by the light of the half moon above. I ran my tongue over my lips and cleared my throat. *I hate this varmint more than anyone else in the Rockies*, I thought. But my traitor dick wouldn't buy it. It swelled to full stiffness in my hand, and I felt my balls shift in their sac in anticipation of a good pumping.

McKenzie wrapped his hand around the back of my neck and planted his mouth over mine. His tongue pushed its way into my mouth and proceeded to explore the back of my throat. I tried to jerk my head away, but McKenzie held on tight. Instinctively my tongue pushed into his mouth and returned the kiss. Off in the distance I heard the sound of men shouting. Someone must have won big at the gaming fire. McKenzie wrapped his hand around my dick and stroked it slowly. I was at that stage of drunkenness where I felt so light I could float. It was only McKenzie's calloused hand around my dick that kept me anchored to the ground.

McKenzie pulled back and looked at me. For once, his expression wasn't mocking and I could see the hunger in his face. Dick hunger. Hunger for *my* dick. His stroke was rougher now, faster; my balls were swinging in the night air fast enough to stir up a breeze. He loosened his grip and let his own dick slide in next to mine within the circle of his fingers. I stared down at our two dicks squeezed together, and I had to admit it was a mighty purty sight. I pulled his face against mine and kissed him hard again.

McKenzie tugged me to the ground and stretched out on top of me full length. He started grinding his hips against mine in a slow, steady rhythm, his dick poking hard against my belly. My body just kind of took over after that, straining against McKenzie's, rubbing against him til I started having a hard time figuring where my skin ended and his began. With all that squirmin' around, our clothes just sort of fell off of us. I reached around and slid my hands across his ass, squeezing his cheeks, fingering his crack, feeling the pucker of his bunghole. McKenzie lifted his head and looked down at me. The moon gleamed full in his face, and damn if he didn't look like some ol' red wolf high in rut. He reached down and cupped my balls. I half expected him to give a hard squeeze, but he just rolled them in his palm like they was two tender eggs bursting to hatch. "I like a man whose nuts have some heft to them," he growled. His hand slid up to my cock and gave it a squeeze. "It seems like you're just all around naturally big down there, Cyrus."

McKenzie took my left nipple between his teeth and bit. The shock was like a sliver of prairie lightning shooting through my body. He rolled my right nipple between his thumb and forefinger and squeezed hard, while his other hand started stroking my dick. I groaned from the sheer pleasure of it all. His tongue blazed a wet trail down my chest, across my belly and into my bush. I pushed my hips up, arching my back, and McKenzie buried his face into my crotch, his beard tickling my balls, his wet mouth slobbering over my dick. I slid my dick between his lips and hard down his throat. McKenzie took it all in like a true mountain man, his tongue doin' a little jig around my meat that just sent sparks through my body. Well, right about then I forgot all about Green-water Creek, and my losing at gambling, and every other reason I had to hate McKenzie, and decided to just ride this bronco ride out. I started pumping my hips, fucking his face with long, steady strokes, and I let out a groan each time I thrust my dick down into his warm, tight mouth. McKenzie looked up at me, my dick still in his mouth, and I could see the laughter in his eyes. I guessed he thought it was funny how easy it was to knock me off of my high horse. But I never was a man to hold grudges, at least against someone who could suck dick as good as McKenzie.

Still, something about his smugness riled me good. I decided to fight fire with fire. "Swing around," I grunted. I didn't have to say it twice. McKenzie shifted his body around and over me so that when I looked up all I could see was his thick dick and low hangin' balls above my face. I buried my nose in them and breathed in deep that ripe, gamey smell. Well, damn if I didn't just about swoon away. If the traders could bottle the smell of McKenzie's balls, they wouldn't need to haul their watered-down whiskey over from St. Louis. I sucked the fleshy red pouch into my mouth and gave it a good washing. It tasted like it needed one. McKenzie gave out a long sigh and then went back to feeding on my dick. As I sucked on his nuts, I wrapped my hand around his dick and stroked it long and fast. McKenzie sighed again, only this time it sounded more like a groan. I squeezed his dick good, feeling its warmth spread through my hand, and slid my tongue up the short hairy path to his asshole. I buried my face in his cheeks and licked his bunghole good. McKenzie's groan was long and trailing, and he missed a beat while sucking my dick. His own dick was slippery with pre-cum, and my hand slid up and down the meaty shaft like bear grease on a skillet.

McKenzie swung around so that he was sitting on my chest facing me. His dick stuck straight up, fat, red, and shiny from my slobber and his precum. "Drop your balls in my mouth," I growled. I swear, I just couldn't get enough of them. McKenzie shifted his body and soon I was tonguing his nuts again. He reached behind me and started stroking my dick, all the time slapping my face with his dick hard enough to make my cheeks sting.

All right, McKenzie, I thought. *You asked for it.* I worked a finger up his ass, up to the last joint, and commenced to finger fuckin' him good. Looking up, with McKenzie's nuts in my mouth, the dark prick in my face, seeing McKenzie's sweat-streaked face look back at me across all that muscled torso, I could see that I'd wiped that grin off of him good. His mouth was pulled back in a snarl, and that cool, blue look in his eyes had given way to a mean, desperate light. His hand was a blur now as he stroked his meat. I shoved my finger hard up his hole and dug in. That did the trick, all right. McKenzie threw back his head and let out a groan fit to raise the dead. Jizz squirted out of his dick, splattering against my face. I opened my mouth for the last drops, rolling them around with my tongue, savoring McKenzie's creamy load. McKenzie kept on pumping my dick with his fist and it warn't more than a couple of seconds more that I felt my own load coming down the pike. Well, I just thrashed and bucked and McKenzie had to hold on for dear life til my load was pretty much squirted out. Finally I lay still, panting. McKenzie stretched out on top of me and licked the rest of his cum off my face.

"Damn if my load ain't 90 proof too," he grinned.

I had to grin too, "I can't think of a more fun way of getting drunk," I said. We both laughed, though I wasn't quite easy about it. I was so used to hating McKenzie that it didn't seem quite right to be horsing around with him like this.

McKenzie seemed to sense this. His eyes narrowed speculatively. "Well, Cyrus," he drawled. "Are we square, or do you still feel like there's unfinished business between us?"

I thought about this for a second. "I'm willing to let bygones be bygones, McKenzie," I said slowly. "But if you start nosing around my trapping areas again, it'll be your scraggly red pelt I'll be selling for a bottle of whiskey at the next rendezvous."

McKenzie grinned but he didn't say anything about backing off. In fact, he didn't say anything at all. He just pulled on his pants, winked at me and rambled back towards the gaming fire. I had a feeling my run-ins with McKenzie were far from over.

Back at the campfire, Coyote was just getting ready to bed down. His face didn't show much expression, but I could tell by the gleam in his eye that sleep was the last thing on his mind. I could just feel my bunghole pucker happily at the plowin' it was about to get, the one thing McKenzie had neglected to give me. I undressed eagerly and slid in under the buffalo skin next to Coyote. Coyote wrapped his arms around me and pulled me to him. His thick bull dick pushed against my belly. "I've had enough of these sad, whiskey-sotted varmints," he growled. "Let's head on back to the mountains first thing sunrise, okay?"

I kissed him lightly. "That's fine by me, Coyote," I grinned. The sounds of shouts and gunshots echoed in the night. The boys were getting frisky out there. Coyote returned my kiss, and then we settled down to the serious business of getting my ass plowed.

BOOKS FROM LEYLAND PUBLICATIONS / G.S PRESS